ISBN: 978-1-948261-47-0
Library of Congress Control Number: 2021920629

Editing and Proofreading: Diane Austin and Rose Albano
Design: Christa I-have-the-coolest-middle-name (Echo) Mella
Cover Photos: Donald Giannatti
Bio Photo: Rose Albano

Visit Foster's website! www.FosterKinn.com.

BANYAN · TREE · PRESS

Published 2021 by Banyan Tree Press,
an imprint of Hugo House Publishers, Ltd.
Denver Colorado, Austin Texas.

FOSTER KINN

THE TRUTH

A Gathering of Short Stories

BANYAN · TREE · PRESS
an imprint of
Hugo House Publishing, Ltd.
Denver Colorado, Austin Texas

ACCLAIM FOR
THE TRUTH: A GATHERING OF SHORT STORIES

"When Foster Kinn opens the throttle, his prose opens up, and the wind in your hair and the smile of the sage rush by just as fast! He suspends any thought of our disbelief that we aren't right there riding along with him."

Ronald Joseph Kule, Acclaimed Biographer and Novelist

While this is primarily a work of fiction, '*The Truth*' is indeed grounded in reality. Once I started reading this book, I could not put it down! Foster's in-depth knowledge of the motorcycle lifestyle is evident throughout his tales, and he tells stories that will engage any reader from the first paragraph. '*The Truth*' is definitely a must-read for any fiction fan.

Bryan "HiWayFlyer" Hall, Long Distance Biker,
Whiskey Drinker, and Author of "Life Behind Bars" HiWayFlyer.com

"Kinn's style of writing is captivating. He paints a clear picture of each character with his cleverly put together words that also bring us some important life lessons. I could not put the book down and actually read through all the stories into the early hours of the morning. A definite must read if you seek a fun and easy to read experience."

Nick Howarth, executive consultant, author of the bestseller "War in Peace."

"Foster Kinn's stories are the twisty-turny stories of adventures we wished we'd lived. They speak of a devotion to freedom; the sensation of an open road ahead that leads only to tomorrow; to integrity and friendship and kindness. There's a smattering of violence to some of the stories, but all within a framework of violence that was well earned. When the hero of each tale and his new or old friends slide through curves or open up the throttle on an Arizona-straight highway, your senses hum with the same smells and sounds that they experience. The emotions are real and never fail to strike the reader vividly. More, please."

Karen Hadley, Researcher, writer, adventurer, lover of
wilderness and cats, author of more than three million words.

"I loved it! Thoroughly enjoyed the last story ... how interesting!"

Linda Ferguson, Serial entrepreneur, marketing maven, coach and strategist

"5 STARS! Someone dropped a gem by the roadside. Well, pick it up! Its a bit of a risk to post 12 (or 13) very different stories ... Not this time! After some I cried. Different tears, joy, happiness, sadness and loss. But after each one of those I was left refreshed ... amazing! Some transported me to other times/other places, chin dropping vistas and worlds. Other stories left me smiling knowingly to myself as if Foster and I were sharing a very personal and spiritual belief ... and we were! This anthology is and forever will be a pure treasure and a treat! ENJOY!"

Walter M. Hugo, fellow author and time traveler

"Wow! Just gobbled up your short stories in one savory bite and swallowed a whole lotta local color and inside heart-throbs all at the same time."

Carol Worthey, Contemporary Classical Composer, Painter,
Author of the acclaimed book "Crumb: The Secret of The Riddle."

"Last night I read the first two stories from *The Truth: a Gathering of Short Stories*, and it was the most fun I'd had in days! Best thing I've read in a loooonnng time! All time favs! The fellow who dies/was dying – very sad and poignant. *My Little Girl* is an amazing story of redemption. Other stories had me laughing. I can't get enough of Kinn's writing!"

Big Red

"I love short stories when they make you think, make you laugh, and make you look at the world through slightly screwed lens. *The Truth: a Gathering of Short Stories by Foster Kinn* ticks every box. It is a book for traveling or for those lazy afternoons when you just want to smile along with a great story. These are truly fun to read. Damned nice book!"

Donald Giannatti, Creative Director, Visual/Content Strategy,
Mentor About *"Darlene and the Mossberg."*

It's not nice to make a hard-ass Vietnam Vet/retired police Sergeant get teary-eyed. Stop that. (Very good story!)

WT Smith, Biker Nonpareil, Patrol Sargent,
Dutchess County Sheriff's Office (retired)

CONTENTS

I dedicate this book to my very first riding partner, Vic Sagerquist.

May you forever ride in Peace, my friend.

THE
TRUTH

A Gathering of Short Stories

FOSTER KINN

PROLOGUE

Name's Foster.
Biker, loner, occasional philosopher.
Lover, reluctant fighter, invisible man.
I've experienced things everyone should experience,
Felt things everyone should feel,
Seen things everyone should see.
Lightning bugs in the Everglades, cicadas in the swamplands;
Weddings, babies being born, kids playing in the mud;
The burn at the end of the last cigarette.
Storms across the Sierra Nevada that come from Hell itself,
Lightning above the timberline,
Thunder so lusty it stops the hands of time.
Lows as deep as the Grand Canyon,
Highs as high as the Rockies,
Mysteries as mysterious as the Mississippi.
Misty morning dawns, nights so dark they make you blind;
Summers so hot that you feel your soul evaporating,
Winters so cold that your bones don't warm up for a year.
Gray days, moonless nights, and lonesome backroads
Where your engine's roar echoes through everything.
Poetry, prose, and music that make everything as it should be.
The touch of a good woman.
I play the wind, laugh at death.
Behind me, I leave mile after mile.
The road is my mistress – someday, perhaps, my demise.

DEVIL AND ANGEL

Taverns, bars, saloons – never could figure out the difference – are, on the whole, safe places. Antagonisms are rare, fights almost unheard of, though I've seen both. But then, I've visited a thousand or more.

If you want to be accurate about it, per day around the world (hundreds of thousands of places, probably over a million), the percentage of antagonisms and fights in taverns, bars, and saloons is minuscule.

So imagine my surprise when, three years ago, I rolled into the parking lot of a tavern on the east side of Fayetteville, Arkansas and saw the following.

———⁓———

She was in the dirt parking lot next to her Harley Softail Heritage facing five bikers, four big ones and a skinny guy a couple of inches under five feet. She was yelling, pointing fingers, and insulting their mommas. Unleashing hell and damnation. The bikers kept trying to laugh but could never quite get there.

It was a pretty day with clouds giving the sky a gentle contour. A little on the cool side with a soft and warm breeze now and again. The life-giving scent of the rosemary bushes that lined all across the front of the tavern mingled with the faint smells of dust and gasoline. A red-tailed hawk screamed once then flew away.

I took a good and long view. She was on the small side. Compact. Tight clothes down and up, headband the color of drying blood, dangling silver earrings that looked like Aphrodite. Long and wavy hair as black as a raven's, sharp and gently sloping nose, long eyelashes, high cheekbones, perfectly curved lips.

Speaking of Aphrodite, that's who she reminded me of. Except for the wrath coming out of her mouth, that is.

As Little Lady Aphrodite kept up with the aspersions, the five bikers (four and a half if you take into account the short and skinny one) soon began trying to not laugh. Yep, anger was slowly taking over. Put another way, it was starting to go the way of ugly.

I had no idea what started it all, of course, but whatever it was, it was five, or four and a half, against one and I'm the kind of guy who sides with the underdog. The thing was, there was no way I was going to take on five, or four and a half, bikers myself even if Little Lady Aphrodite stood by me.

Then I remembered something my daddy taught me and my granddaddy taught him: If it's a contest between boredom and antagonism or anger, boredom wins every time. So I walked over, stood in front of Little Lady Aphrodite and faced the bikers, looking as bored as I could.

Silence.

The super short one spoke up. "She yer sister or something?" He chuckled once. No one else did.

The biggest one gave me a hard glare. "None of your fucking business." I nodded once, slowly. An uneasy silence followed that seemed way longer than I'm sure it was. Then, "Get the fuck out."

Then I remembered something else my daddy taught me: The best way to express boredom is a big ol' yawn. In fact, he claimed that being able to yawn whenever you needed to was a skill that's as valuable as shooting a rifle.

So that's what I did. A big, big ol' yawn. A damn good one, too. Long and lazy. Immediately, all four and a half bikers' faces conveyed the same thing: What the hell?

Who the hell? Huh?

One by one, the seconds slowly passed, like pouring cold syrup on flapjacks. I kept standing there, looking all bored, eyes and mouth drooping down, like when your girlfriend takes you shopping for spatulas and frying pans.

It wasn't long, maybe a half minute or so, before the big one said, "Fuck it," and walked back into the tavern. The rest of them followed

Tell ya what, my daddy and granddaddy were wise men. I'm thinking they would have been proud of me.

I turned around and, good lord!, that chick was still pissed. Looked at me like I was a rabid coyote.

She rasped, "What? I'm supposed to thank you now?"

"Well …"

"Because little ol' me can't protect myself?" she sneered. "And I need a man to save me?"

"Uh …"

"And now, what? You want me to get on my knees and give you a blow job?"

I half-smiled. "I'll admit the thought did cross my mind."

Whack! She slapped me. And it wasn't one of those pre-puberty girly-girl slaps, no sirree. She hit me with the heel of her hand upside my cheekbone. It hurt. I stood still while the pain subsided. "You know, I was just joking."

"Fuck you."

I knew I shouldn't have said it, but I couldn't help myself. "That thought crossed my mind, too."

Whack! Another shot to my cheek. That one really hurt. Took longer for the pain to go away. "You know, that, too, was just a joke."

"Fuck you again."

Again, I did something stupid. Raised my eyebrows and put my hands out, palms up. "Well?"

Whack! Steel-toed boot square on my shin. I started thinking I was going to need an ambulance. "Okay, okay. Look, you don't have to thank me. I just saw five, or four and a half, against one. Didn't like the odds."

She chuckled. "Four and a half. That's funny."

"Thought it was a pretty good line myself."

In a flash, she's back to being pissed. "Oh. And now you're mister smart guy?"

I sighed, thinking I should change the subject. I looked around. "Sure is a pretty day."

She glared like a scorned trophy wife.

"The smell of those rosemary bushes. Man, oh man."

She leaned back and crossed her arms. I swear, her earrings did look like Aphrodite. So did she.

One more try. "How do you like that Heritage?"

Not a word. She was still leaning back, arms still crossed, looking at me like I had the worst breath in the world and my hair was weaved with dead cockroaches. Obviously, the conversation wasn't going to go any further than it had, which was essentially nowhere.

Besides, I was incredibly thirsty, and a tall, cold glass of lemonade in that tavern was calling my name, so I put out my hand, smiled, and said, "Elijah. Elijah Jones."

She waited before she took my hand. Waited longer to say, "Zoe."

I nodded once then walked toward the tavern. She called to me. "Hey. Mr. Elijah Jones."

I turned around. Her eyes darted left, right, at the sky, at the dirt, then she looked straight at me. The right side of her mouth flicked outward. She actually looked downright demure. "Thanks."

"Sure thing, Aphrodite."

As I entered the tavern, I heard the roar from her Heritage as she took off.

———✿———

I sat at the bar and ordered a lemonade. In the mirror behind the bar, I could see the four and a half bikers sitting at a table far to my right. They were talking and laughing and seemed to have totally forgotten about the face-off in the parking lot. Except for the super short and skinny one. He kept staring at me, hate-filled like a feral cat. Didn't bother me, though. They finally left.

After finishing the lemonade, I drank a few beers, then went back to lemonade along with a plate of fries. Chatted with the bartender, Rick, about the upcoming baseball playoffs. A little politics. Blonds, brunettes, redheads. Habits we licked and those we couldn't. A couple of old-as-the-hills-and-twice-as-dusty jokes that I can't remember. It was an honest series of conversations, meaning Rick wasn't just trying to get a big tip. I left him one anyway.

I took off going east. Wandered around some backroads, which is where you truly find the magic of the Ozarks. The trees were thick, the shadows grew long, then longer. I caught glimpses of the Buffalo River a few times, finally found a place to park, then walked down to it. Sat on a rock and listened to the lazy waters.

"Are you fucking following me?"

Little Lady Aphrodite? It can't be.

"Well? Are you?"

I looked around. Couldn't see her.

"Hey. I'm talking to you, asshole."

I stood up and looked around some more. Finally looked up and, whaddya know, she's sitting in a tree.

"Well, if it isn't Little Lady Aphrodite."

Again I got that scorned trophy wife glare. "Why do you call me that? Wasn't she like a ancient Greek whore or something?"

"Well, that's sort of what I heard but that's not why. Your earrings remind me of her." I waited. "And she was drop-dead gorgeous."

"Hmph." She looked away.

After sitting back down, I said, "I'm not following you."

We sat in silence long enough to smoke three cigarettes. The sun was getting close to the horizon and the flying insects were multiplying. Before leaving, I looked up at Zoe and smiled. "Have a fine evening, Aphrodite."

———&———

The oversized summer sun had just touched the horizon when I got a room in a cheap but clean motel in Hollister, Missouri, just south of Branson. A half hour later, I heard a jackhammer-like pounding on my door. I opened it.

It was Zoe. Still pissed. "Why are you following me?"

"Uh, I'm not following you."

"Then why are you where I am?"

I stuck my head out the door. Sure enough, three parking spaces down was Zoe's Heritage. "When did you check in?"

"Just now."

"Right. Well, I checked in a half hour ago, so how could I be following you?"

The lasers coming out of her eyes! "Fuck you." And she walked away.

An hour later, another pounding on my door startled me out of my early evening reverie.

Zoe again. "Take me to dinner."

"Uh, well, I already got pizza delivered. It was a two-for-one so there's a lot left if

you want some. If you like pepperoni and sausage, that is. And root beer."

"So that's how you do it?"

"Do what?"

"Get women in your room for a couple of slices of pizza then fuck 'em."

I closed my eyes. Sighed. "No."

We stared at each other before I opened the door wide and pointed at the table.

"So do you want some pizza and root beer or not."

She hesitated. "Fine." She brushed past me like I was a castoff coat on a rack in a thrift store.

"But you have to promise not to hit me or kick me."

"Not gonna promise anything."

I nodded once. "Figured that."

She went at the pizza like a starving mama-dog. Ate her first slice in something like

ten seconds. And downed a half liter of root beer.

I let her swallow the last of it. "When was the last time you ate?"

She froze and stared then, ignoring my question, started on a second slice. "Why'd you get thin crust?"

"I prefer it. So when was the last time you ate?"

"None of your business."

I nodded. We sat in silence. She continued eating and drinking while I pulled up a playlist on my laptop. Zac Brown, Alan Jackson, Chris Stapleton, a few others.

Toward the end of the Zac Brown track she asked, "Why do you listen to that?"

"I like it."

"It's sad."

"*Bittersweet?* Yeah, it's definitely sad." I thought about it as the last chord faded away. "Beautiful, though."

She nodded then looked to the side, like she was yearning for a release from some past anguish.

Alan Jackson's *Good Time* came on. She smiled a few times then asked, "You like to line dance?"

"I do."

"Me, too."

"Haven't been in a long time."

"Me, neither."

Chris Stapleton's *Tennessee Whiskey* came on next. During the guitar solo, she scrunched her eyebrows. "How does he do that?"

"Do what?"

"Sing like that."

"Haven't a clue. He's one of a kind. I mean, everybody's one of a kind, but he's way out there one of a kind." I listened closely to the third chorus. "Y'know, in all of music, there's no better track to make love to."

She looked at me, forlorn, like a puppy at the pound. "I'm a bitch, huh."

I studied that exquisite face and looked into eyes behind which lay impenetrable emotions that bespoke a sorrow-filled spirit. "I'll tell you something, Zoe. All good women have a little hellcat in them." I smiled. "Of course, you have a lot more than a little."

I was half-expecting a slap in the face or a swift kick in the shins, but she just kept up with this downhearted basset hound look. Finally, she said, "Gotta go back to my room." She stopped in the doorway looking out at the parking lot. "Thanks for the pizza and the root beer, Mr. Elijah Jones."

It was around eight the following morning when I finished loading up the bike. I was in my room checking to make sure I didn't leave anything behind when there was another knock at my door, this one civilized.

Yeah. Zoe. "I have to stay another night."

"Uh, okay."

"I'm low on money. Need to stay with you. Just one night."

I thought about that, the advantages of it. I mean, she *was* hot. Really hot. Then I remembered those two slaps in the face and the kick to my shins. "Well, I was getting ready to head on out."

"Just one night."

I took a deep breath. The air was getting warm. "Zoe, there's just one bed in this room. If you and I spend a night in the same room and in the same bed, we will have sex."

"You can sleep on the floor."

"Uhhh, no." For some reason, the noises from the street began to bother me.

"Okay look, I'll pay for your room for one more night then I gotta take off. That work?"

"No. You need to stay."

"Why? You piss off another four and a half bikers?"

A smile flickered across her face. "No."

"Then why?"

She shrugged her shoulders. Silence.

I sighed, looked at the traffic, then back at Zoe. "Okay, the rooms are forty-five bucks. I'll pay for both of ours. Then maybe you can tell me why you need me here."

And just like that, she walked back to her room. Not even a thank you.

I paid for the rooms then unloaded my bike. All in all, staying another day wasn't a bad idea because the surrounding area was lush and aching for some loud pipes. I figured I'd spend the day riding, which is what I did. As I rolled out of the parking lot, I could see her out of the corner of my eyes, watching me through the curtains.

The backroads around Hollister were old but, owing to the lack of traffic, in pretty darn good shape. Like I said, the trees and bushes were lush and thick with shadows and secrets, the birds and insects like messengers of the wisdom from the ancient hills.

There were a number of sharp curves, but I didn't push hard through them. Back then was when I began to more and more view roads as living entities, built to handle certain vehicles at certain speeds, and that if I continually found that certain speed along with the ideal lean angle, I could ride for hours never using my brakes. When I did that, I entered a world of balance, of harmony, the roar from my engine the masculine hymn of freedom.

I stopped for coffee and a muffin at a gas station in Seneca. While sitting on the bench outside, my thoughts turned to Zoe. Where did she come from? Where was she going? And why?

I mean, I knew why I lived on the road, but it seemed she was doing something else, that the road was nothing more than a bothersome route that led to some destination or several. Well, if she decided to tell me, she would. If not, then not. Either way, it was, at the least, another road story for a book I'd never write.

The day seemed to rush by and I had to fill the tank only once. Sure, if you're riding freeways and highways, that doesn't make for much mileage but it means a damn good amount when you're riding nothing but hills and crooked roads. I was pretty darn tired when I got to my room and again ordered pizza and root beer.

Another knock at my door. Zoe yet again. "You just got some pizza."

"Another two-for-one. Same as last night."

Without a word or hesitation, she rushed past me, sat at the table, then began devouring the pizza. And much of the root beer. She'd just started her second slice when she said, "Play those songs again."

This time we just listened. Ate and drank. No words.

As the playlist wandered into other artists, I wandered to my laptop and wrote some emails. Zoe had already wandered off into another world with the same sadness I'd seen the night before.

Some time later, she got up to leave. Standing in the doorway, she said, "Thank you for dinner." She flashed a smile. "Good night, Mr. Elijah Jones."

"And may flights of angels sing thee to thy rest, Aphrodite."

She stared, eyes as wide as chestnuts. "You just make that up?"

"Shakespeare. Hamlet."

"Oh."

Zoe knocked on my door at seven-thirty the following morning. "We should get breakfast."

"Aha! Are we going to be back in time to check out?"

"You will. I already did."

"Okay. Where do you want to go?"

"Some place downtown."

"I'll follow."

Chelsea's Diner was my kind of place. The drone of a dozen conversations, plates and silverware clanking, waitresses calling out orders, the smells of coffee and frying bacon and ham. I waited for Zoe to tell me why she wanted me to stick around, but she offered nothing.

After ordering, she got up to go to the ladies room. Her purse hung on the back of her chair, but she grabbed only one strap as she walked away and ended up yanking the chair down with a slap-bang. Half the purse's contents fell out. She didn't notice a folded piece of old paper slide all the way under my chair. I helped her pick up everything else, then she headed to the ladies room.

21

I picked up the folded paper and put it in my back pocket. When Zoe came back, I excused myself to go to the bathroom. It was there that I unfolded that piece of paper.

It was a photocopy of a four-year-old newspaper item, which had to do with the trial of an alleged rape of an eighteen-year-old girl, Piper Hatfield. The defendant was a young and newly rich guy named Tommy Talbot, who owned a car dealership in Southern Georgia.

The judge had dismissed a bunch of hard evidence, one of which was Piper's underwear, which had Tommy Talbot's DNA on it. Another was Piper's blood test, which had a fair amount of a date rape drug in it. It seems that a well-meaning but inexperienced secretary at the police station had possibly broken the chain of evidence.

Other things, too, like three eyewitnesses who had seen Piper in Tommy Talbot's car that night. And another group of young people who had seen her forced into it.

Evidently, a moonless night, a couple of beers, and the passage of time will cloud over people's memories, making them ineffectual under cross examination.

Add to all that a high-priced lawyer, an over-worked public prosecutor, and a slackminded judge, and you end up with a verdict of not guilty.

Piper had to be Zoe's daughter. Had to be. And she had been raped and the guy who did it was free to roam around. I don't have any kids, never been married, but putting myself in Zoe's position as best as I could, it was easy to understand her loathing for men.

I walked back to our table but before sitting down, I watched the increasingly thick traffic for a few moments. I sat. Closed my eyes. Listened to the cacophony of a diner at breakfast time. I opened my eyes and as I had the evening before, studied her face.

Ravishing and fetching.

She suspiciously asked, "What?"

"What's your last name?"

"Hatfield."

I bore my eyes into her. "You're looking for him."

She narrowed her eyes. "Who?"

"Tommy Talbot."

The hellfire coming out of her bore right through me. She rasped, "How do you know him?"

"I…"

"Friend of yours? He send you after me?"

My first thought was that it was a good thing that the table between us was bolted to the floor. Instead of answering, I pulled the folded paper out of my pocket and held it in the air between us. She grabbed it like a falcon on a field mouse.

She then put her head in her hands and sobbed for several minutes. "So you know."

After some time, she wiped away the tears and blew her nose. She traced her finger across a steak knife, brushing the remnants of ham off of the serrated edge. "I can find Tommy any time I want. I'm not looking for him." Then she said mostly to herself, "Not yet, anyway." That "not yet" sounded ominous.

"So you're looking for Piper and that's why you're on the road."

"Yeah. She ran away after the trial. People called her a liar. Tommy's wife spread rumors all over about her being a whore. Lost all her friends.

"She's smart so I figured she probably changed her name right off but just to make sure I checked every Piper Hatfield in the country first." She shook her head slightly.

"Nothing. Since then I've been trying all the possible name combinations I can think of. First one was Hattie Paul."

A second set of tears began rolling down her cheeks. "When she was little, Hattie Paul was what she called her favorite doll. Pauline is her middle name."

She looked at me. "I sold everything. The house, the car, most of my clothes, all my shoes. Refrigerator, TVs, furniture, everything except the bike and a half-week's worth of clothes. When I had all that money, I figured that if I stuck to a strict budget, I'd have five years."

Outside, the traffic compressed more and more. The commuters grew testy.

Several horns honked. I asked, "How many years has it been?"

"Four." She stared into a vast emptiness. "I miss her so much. Her dad, Charlie, my husband, died before she was born so it's always been just us two. 'Two together forever' we used to say."

I waited several moments. "She never called you?"

"She couldn't. Got nasty phone calls and messages day and night so I changed my number before two days passed. Didn't realize till afterwards how stupid it was."

Her wet eyelashes glistened, her voice faltered. "People called me a whore, too. A 'madam' for my daughter. Was about to lose my job."

She looked out the window and followed a few birds in flight. "I thought I'd find her pretty fast and end up with enough money to start over. I took a bike mainly because she always imagined riding her own some day and I figured I'd give it to her when we reconnected."

She wiped away the tears. "I call up the ones with listed numbers. Have to visit anyone with an unpublished or unlisted number. I'm trying Pauline Pipers now."

I sighed, thinking about it all. The injustice and the tragedy. Outside, the persistent halt-and-go traffic radiated an unnatural heat through the front doors that slowly dissipated the morning chill. "So why make me spend an extra day here?"

Then it hit me. I leaned back and cocked my head to the right. "Last night was the last night of the month and you'd already burned through your monthly budget."

She nodded.

"And you figured a free breakfast was a good way to start the new month."

She scrunched her eyebrows and looked down at her crumpled napkin. "How'd you know?"

I shrugged my shoulders, hands out, palms up.

Silent minutes passed. Then more. At last, without preamble, she stood up. "Gotta get to Wichita by sunset. Stop in Joplin first."

I walked with her to her Heritage. Just before she took off, I said, "Find your daughter, Zoe. Take care of yourself and find her."

She half-smiled, her eyes squinting against the morning sun. "Thank you for breakfast Mr. Elijah Jones."

I watched her ride away. All the way down the street then around a left turn.

EPILOGUE

Looking back, I maybe should have offered to ride with her and help. Sure, she was mostly a hellcat, but she was also a mother looking for her daughter. I couldn't personally relate to that, but the fact that she had given up everything to do so overshadowed her lack of, shall I say, social graces.

Then I remembered other things. The sweet way she said "Thank you" for the pizza and root beer and the soft way she said, "Mr. Elijah

Jones." And at the end of the standoff with the bikers, she had changed her manner and said "thank you" then, too.

And that forlorn, puppy-dog look.

I figured that that sweetness and softness was the way she truly was. That everything else, the slaps and the kicking and the vicious verbal attacks, was an unnatural addendum to her true personality.

Now, I'm not a believer in destiny or fate or whatever, but I do know that there are times when two people, even those who just met, will meet again. Why? Don't know and don't need to. And that's why I knew right then that Zoe "Aphrodite" Hatfield and I would cross paths in the future.

And, in fact, we did. But that's a whole other story. Much longer, too. For another time, perhaps.

END

SHOT

One of the senses you develop when riding a motorcycle is to know when someone else is having trouble. It usually takes a while to mature but we all eventually get it and it's a good sense to have.

One day while riding south on San Francisquito Canyon in Southern California, that sense rose up through my thoughts, becoming either a premonition or a promise. Still haven't figured out which.

I first saw them about a half mile away. Two ladies standing next to their bikes in a turnout. And though they weren't actually doing anything, they were broadcasting having trouble like a 50,000 watt radio signal.

I pulled over. One of them, Naomi, was stiff-scared, like a sinner waiting for the Second Coming. The other one, Brenda, did all the talking.

Brenda told me the problem was with Naomi's bike, an 883 Ironhead. She took me over to it, stepped on the back brake and it went down like a ten pound sack of potatoes dropped off the back of a pickup. Damn.

I got out my magnifying glass then looked over the entire brake line, starting at the top. Then I saw it. Right there, just past the peg.

A vertical slice, clean and straight and covered with brake fluid. It substantiated a deliberate intent to harm.

I looked at Naomi and figured that, as anxiety-ridden as she already was, she was in no state of mind to hear about someone sabotaging her bike. Besides, I was a stranger and news like that should come from someone she knows and trusts. So to make a good show of it, I inspected the rest of the brake line.

I walked over to Naomi. "So your back brake went out, huh?" She nodded with a sort of hurt pride. "How long have you been riding?"

"First time in twenty years."

I slowly nodded and looked at Brenda. "You?"

"Since I was eight."

I slowly nodded again. "Where do you ladies live?"

Brenda glanced at Naomi. "Valencia, a half mile past the end of San Francisquito.

My husband's Naomi's brother."

Again I nodded. "Okay, this is what we're gonna do. Brenda, you ride my bike; Naomi, you ride Brenda's Sportster, and I'll ride yours."

Naomi looked skeptical. "Is that even possible?"

"Oh yeah. Not ideal, but it can be done." I looked around and felt that marvelous mixture of fading winter cold and burgeoning springtime warmth. "We'll be going pretty darn slow so we'll need the emergency lights on. I'll lead. Naomi, you're behind me; Brenda, you take up the rear."

We took off and I was honestly surprised at how well that old Ironhead handled.

Until a half mile later when the front brakes went out. Damn again. We kept going and it wasn't a problem, what with engine braking and all, until we got past that stop sign and into some traffic. I went really slow then. So slow that I could stop the bike with my feet.

When we got to their place, I coasted right into the garage. As soon as I dismounted, I heard Naomi yelling in a righteous fit of anger to no one in particular.

"Brian's the biggest shit mechanic ever! Gonna kill him!" Then in a sneering voice, "He said the brakes were good, real good. Fucking asshole." (I swear I could see smoke coming out of her nose.)

She pulled out her cell. I went over. "Wait, wait, wait, hold on a minute." I looked at the other guy there. "You're Brenda's husband and Naomi's brother?"

"Name's James."

"Okay. Name's Caleb. Friends call me Cab. Know much about bikes?"

"A little."

I've been riding long enough to know that that's the answer someone gives when they know just about everything.

I turned to Naomi. "Let me show James what happened before you call Brian. He'll be able to explain it a lot better than me."

Naomi's face softened. "Okay." I had just turned to go when she said, "Hey." I turned around. She was half smiling. "Thanks."

"Sure thing."

Brenda and Naomi went into the house and when James and I got into the garage, I stood next to Naomi's Ironhead, staring at him.

He looked at me with one eye half shut. "What?"

I took a deep breath. "Well, first off, the front brakes went out about a half mile after we took off."

"Uh-huh."

"And uh, there's nothing wrong with the brake job."

"Uh-huh."

"So uh, the back brake line was sliced. Probably the front, too." I waited a few seconds. "Hold on." I got my magnifying glass then showed him where the slice was. He checked out the front brake line and found a similar slice there. Man, the savagery coming out of that man's eyes!

I continued, "There's something else."

"Uh-huh."

"A fingerprint just in front of the bottom slice." James looked again, saw it, then glared into space. I continued. "This is at least attempted manslaughter. If the police lift the print, they can probably find out who did it."

"I know who did it."

I stopped breathing. He looked into the dark corners of the garage. "Naomi's ex, Beanie." He continued staring for some minutes. "We're not calling the police." He turned to me. "You okay with that?"

I held his gaze for some moments. "I am."

———— ✴ ————

Naomi and Brenda were at the kitchen table. I sat on Naomi's left, James sat across from her. He said, "Three things. First is the front brakes went out a half mile after you, Brenda and Cab here took off."

Naomi looked at me, mouth open. "You rode without brakes? You could've died!"

I half smiled. "Well uh, no. We were going pretty darn slow."

"But still that was dangerous!" She looked at me like I was some sort of hero.

James then said, "Second thing: There's nothing wrong with the brake job."

"Okay." She hesitated. "What was it?"

He waited. "That's the third thing. Brake lines were sliced."

"Sliced? What does that mean?"

"Brake lines are rubber. They were sliced with a razor blade or an X-acto knife. All the brake fluid leaked out and without brake fluid the brakes won't work."

Naomi's look slowly became more and more horrified. "But who...."

"You know who."

In a shaken voice, Naomi quietly said, "Beanie." She began to cry.

Brenda took Naomi to the couch and just held her so she could get it all out.

———

James was a big man, well over six feet tall. Big hands, muscle-filled arms, steelbeam strong. The rest of him was filled out a bit but he walked with a jaguar's gait, stealthy and quiet.

He pulled out his cell. "Get the boys together. All of 'em. Important. Saturday at one at France's place." He hit the hang-up button so hard he about crushed his phone. He nodded to the back porch and I followed him outside.

We sat in silence for a while. A cricket chirped once. Then again. It was comfortably cool. Without a preamble, he told me Naomi's short history.

"She's a smart gal except for always choosing the wrong guy. Either drugs or the drink or the carousing. Whatever the reason, it always ended bad. She's carefree and guys take it for being stupid. That and those giant tits – I'm sure you noticed – and she's like a picnic watermelon to ants.

"Two years ago, she got married for the fourth time. At first, Beanie seemed okay but, to be honest, I never really trusted him. No drink or drugs, but he always had this knife-in-the-back thing about him."

James took a big breath. Looked at the silhouettes of the backyard trees against an orange sunset. "The last three months were bad, but it started before that. Made her quit work, stay at home, took her phone away. Treated her like trash. Don't know when the hitting started but it had to be going on for a while. Maybe all the time. Brenda and me didn't know 'cause we hardly ever saw her."

He took another deep breath. "Brenda went to see her once for lunch. Just popped in out of the blue. Beanie wasn't there, lucky for him. Brenda's got a temper.

"Anyway, that's when she saw the bruise on Naomi's neck. She figured there were others and wanted to see them. Naomi didn't want to show her but, well, Brenda's Brenda and when she gets her mind set, there's no changing it."

He rubbed his shoes together. "Brenda brought her back to our place and made me look at 'em. They were all over. Except for her face and forearms. I was so firedup pissed I couldn't breathe.

"Naomi calmed me down but I still wanted to fuck that asshole up. She stayed with us from that day and as time went on, she calmed me down more and more.

Got me to the point where I wasn't gonna do anything." He smacked his fist into his palm. "Should have. Should've gone over and smashed his head in."

His eyes flicked to the north at the mournful sound of a mockingbird. When it quit crying, we sat in silence.

James looked straight at me. "Naomi filed for divorce and he agreed right away."

He paused. "See. That's suspicious. What kind of man agrees to a divorce straight off?" His upper lip went into a snarl. "One with nothing in his blood but evil."

Again, we sat in silence. Then, "As soon as she moved in, weird things started happening. Small things at first. People stared at her then looked away when she saw them. Friends a little stand-offish. Trouble at work. Not the kinds of things you'd think out of the ordinary but looking back, they were like bright red flares.

"Slowly got worse. Car scored one night. Air let out of her tires. Threatening letters, too. Like those ransom notes you see on a TV show: letters cut out of old magazines. Said things like she'd never be safe, better keep an eye out. Fucked up shit like that.

"It got even worse when she got that old Ironhead. Our friend Brian – good man, good mechanic – did all the work on it and things started getting weird for him, too. Losing work and shit."

I waited then said, "Seems you have it pegged. Who else but her ex?"

"Right."

Again, we sat in silence for some time. He said, "See, the reason calling the police wouldn't do any good, except piss off that piece of shit even more, is just because his fingerprint is there doesn't prove he's the one that cut the lines. Could have been somebody else."

James made a good point. Beanie would get off and end up being even more revengeful.

He looked down and wrung his hands. "Old school justice." He nodded several times. "Old school justice."

———— ∿ ————

The ladies had begun making dinner. Nothing fancy. Microwaved lasagna and salad with a pre-cooked peach pie for dessert. I was invited, which was a good thing because I was damn hungry. We had a little time before the lasagna would be done, so James and Brenda went off to talk about husband and wife matters, which left me and Naomi alone.

We sat on the couch, her at one end, me at the other. She looked at me with a slight, sweet smile. I looked back. Slender, fetching eyes, aquiline nose. Kitten-like pose, little-girl innocence. Not a supermodel type of face but homespun attractive.

And yeah, those giant tits. I could see why guys were attracted to her. I sure as hell was. She said, "I wanna thank you again. You were real brave doing what you did."

"Oh, didn't take much. Just going slow is all."

"But it was brave. Like you saved me."

I could feel my face turning red. "Well okay, then." I raised my eyebrows and bowed slightly. "You're welcome, m'lady."

She giggled. "You're so sweet!"

I half-smiled. "Do my best."

She scooted to my side of the couch. "Hope you like dinner. We didn't have time to actually make anything. Just, you know, the microwave thing."

"Oh, that'll be more than fine. As hungry as I am, I could eat that whole sucker if it was still frozen."

She laughed, her nose scrunching up a little. "Maybe I could make a real dinner for you sometime. Roast beef in a crock pot with red rose potatoes and baby carrots and gravy. I'm real good at gravy."

It was hard to believe but man, oh man, here she was hitting on me. "Sounds like a fine evening."

"Yeah!" She put her arm in mine. "I live in the guest house in the backyard so it could just be us two."

"Now, that sounds real fine."

Dinner came around and with it a pleasant conversation. Dumb jokes, some old, some new, and light laughing. But through it all, I could tell James was a little preoccupied. Me, too. But Brenda was a fine hostess so the atmosphere was mostly relaxed. Naomi seemed to have forgotten all about the brake line issue and was wholesomely charming.

After dessert, it was around 10 p.m., Brenda brought out some blankets and pillows and put them on the couch. She said, "Breakfast is at six. Hope you like hash browns and scrambled eggs."

"My kind of meal."

"Great! We're heading off to bed. You know where the bathroom is, right?"

"I do."

"Okay. Good night."

Naomi just finished up a long yawn. "Guess I better hit the sack, too." She walked over, I stood up, then we hugged real tight. "Thank you, again. You're the best."

"You're welcome, again, Naomi. You have a fine sleep."

———— ❧ ————

I don't know how long it was. Anywhere from an hour to three or four. I woke up as Naomi was pushing the blankets onto the floor. She unbuckled and unzipped my jeans then pulled them and my underwear down past my feet. She was wearing nothing but a muslin top, which she smoothly pulled off. She then began working me like a thousand-dollar-an-hour Vegas hooker.

She climbed on top and we immediately got into a rhythm. Many minutes passed – gawd, did it feel good! – then we sped up, then some more. Some minutes later, it was like a silent explosion, every nerve electric, minds blind with ecstasy.

I stayed inside her as she bent down and kissed me over and over. We kept at it until our breathing and heart rates returned to normal, never speaking a word. She closed her eyes and laid her head on my shoulder. After a while, she raised up, half smiled, climbed off, then walked back to her little, one-room home.

———✴———

Breakfast was a little awkward. Naomi and I did our best to play it cool but we both knew that Brenda had no doubts about what had happened between us the night before.

James? He was still preoccupied. Drumming his fingers, darting his eyes here and there.

I was ready to head on home, but before I got on my bike, I thanked Brenda for her hospitality. When I shook hands with James, he said, "The meeting with the boys is set up for this coming Saturday afternoon. Since you're part of this, thinking you might want to come."

"Wouldn't miss it."

Naomi came over and thanked me for the fifth or sixth time. Kissed me on the cheek then thanked me again. Then she invited me over for dinner on Wednesday, two nights later. Well, after what had happened between us just hours before, there was no way I'd turn down that invitation!

I called Naomi that night. The following night, too. Damn, what a sweet gal! Felt like we were in high school and she was my first real girlfriend and I was her first boyfriend.

I swear, we talked about everything. Books we'd read, teachers we'd had, our families, our political inclinations, favorite sports teams, everything. So much good stuff. I was warmed at how, despite all the troubles she'd endured, she maintained an upbeat attitude about life, that no matter the gray of the past, the future was colorful and full of opportunity.

The only melancholia was when she talked about her ex-boyfriends and exhusbands, especially Beanie. She would have this fatalistic anguish in her voice, like she had somehow failed but didn't know, and would never know why. And every time, I wanted to reach out, tightly hug her and make all those disappointments go away and go away for good.

It was evident that, for whatever reasons, she had made bad choices when it came to the men she allowed into her heart, but it was also true that she absolutely did not deserve to have been treated as she had. She simply wanted a man who returned the honesty and fidelity that she gave him.

We always stopped short of making any future plans. Not that we wouldn't have wanted to, but the reality was that we'd known each other for only a few days and had had just that one silent night together. Without saying it, we both felt there was no need to rush the future.

———

Wednesday rolled around and, man, was I excited! Shaved real close, made sure all my clothes were clean, and even got a haircut. I was to be at Naomi's by five so I took off a little after four. The traffic on Interstate 5 sucked big time, it always does, but I was so damn elated that it didn't affect me in the least.

I was at one of those big urban intersections a couple of blocks from Naomi's place. Right turn lanes, left turn lanes, lights that last for minutes and minutes. My left hand was tired from holding in the clutch, the heat from my engine inexorably curled up, and small beads of sweat formed on my face.

It was then that another biker sense popped up, one that's more prevalent than knowing when someone else is in trouble. And that sense is the one that tells you danger is beginning to show its ugly mug.

The object of my attention was a bright red, totally tricked-out '68 Plymouth Roadrunner across the street, way to my left, facing the opposite direction. He was in his right turn lane, but it seemed like he wasn't interested in turning right. Instead, he kept inching forward like an amateur dragster waiting for the go-light.

Now, I was in my own right-turn lane, right next to the curb, but traffic was such that I couldn't make that turn with any measure of safety. On the corner to my right was a mom and her two children, who were waiting for the WALK signal. The boy, maybe two or three years old, was in a stroller, and holding the lady's hand was a girl about seven or eight.

So there we were. Waiting. With danger a-cropping. The lights finally turned green, the WALK signal glowed, and the lady and her kids entered the crosswalk.

The driver in the Roadrunner screamed out. Instead of turning right, he turned left in front of everyone else, fishtailing across the intersection, tires squealing. He clipped the front of the stroller, lost control, then smashed into a bus bench.

The mom and her daughter were whipped around and went sprawling on theasphalt. They both screamed. The mom lost her grip on the stroller, which miraculously stayed upright and just slowly rolled down the street fifty or so yards before several guys grabbed it.

I immediately parked in the gas station on the corner then ran to the mom and her daughter. They were scraped up some but no bones seemed broken. They were, however, hysterical, especially the mother. A crowd gathered as I began calming them down, something I'm good at.

The little boy was brought back and, having no idea what had just happened, was giggling. And just like that, everything was fine. Except for the scrapes and bruises.

I asked a bystander to get some water bottles out of my saddlebags, with which I began cleaning the mom's and her daughter's road rashes. By then, there were a good thirty people standing about and the mood had gone from all-out shock to thank-god-everyone's-okay.

Everything had been going along smoothly when the driver of the Roadrunner walked over. He looked down at me and barked, "I need some help."

I looked up. His face and hair were half-covered with blood and he was badly rattled but, to be honest, I cared not one whit about him. Without a word, I went back to tending the mom and her daughter.

Again, he spoke up. "Hey. Need some help here."

I ignored him.

"I said I need some help!"

Again, I ignored him.

"Dammit man, I'm covered with blood! Need some help!"

I stood up, walked over to him until there was but inches between our faces, then quite calmly said, "I'm not going to help you because you don't deserve it," then went back to tending the mom and her daughter.

The thirty-some-odd people standing around either nodded or smiled. A few even chuckled. Unfortunately, no one paid him any mind as he walked to his Roadrunner and grabbed a .38 snub-nose.

When he got back, he began shooting. One shot grazed my right rib cage, another was a through-and-through into my left shoulder. I was laid out flat, losing blood like a broken water main. Fortunately, no one else was hit. He got off four, maybe five rounds before a bunch of guys pounced on him.

As I laid there, I watched those guys beat that driver into oblivion. It was gruesome. Blood. Broken bones. Pathetic pleas for mercy. Oh so satisfying. Later, when the police questioned me about it, I said I hadn't seen a thing.

While waiting for the ambulance, a biker and his lady knelt next to me. The biker said, "Name's Tubby, this here's Sue, my lady. If you want, we'll take care of your bike. Live close, space in the garage, give you our numbers."

I nodded. They seemed like reliable folks. Most bikers are. "Thanks. Sounds good."

The ambulances arrived just then. I was pretty much in agony but the nurse put me on a morphine drip right away. Within a minute, I concluded that morphine was the greatest invention in the history of greatest inventions. Funny thing, the pain in my ribs took longer to subside than the one in my shoulder.

What with the ambulance ride, the hospital paperwork, and doctors examining me and all that, it was a good hour and a half before I had some time to myself, though I was still in the emergency room.

My morphine inspired thoughts were swimming, or more like drowning, and most of them had to do with Naomi. She had made dinner. We were going to spend a lustful night together. And I was late. Really late. With not a word from me, she must be worried. Or pissed. Didn't know her well enough to know which.

I got out my cell and called. Brenda answered. "Yeah."

"Uh, hi Brenda. Is Naomi around?"

"Why."

"Um, I need to talk to her."

"Uh-huh."

I wasn't thinking clearly, I knew that, but kept going. "So is she there?" No answer. "Brenda?"

"What."

It wasn't going well. "Look, I just want to talk to Naomi."

"Uh-huh."

"Please?"

I could hear their voices but none of the words. A long minute passed. Finally, Naomi came onto the phone. "What?"

"Oh! Hi Naomi!" No response. "Uh, so I want to apologize." No response. "For not being there." No response. "I'm really sorry." Still no response. It still wasn't going well, what with my veins filled with morphine, but I just couldn't think of anything to say but that I was sorry.

The seconds ticked by. Finally, I managed to say, "Look. There's a good reason."

"Uh-huh."

"Uh … yeah. I'm in the hospital."

Silence. "The hospital?"

"Yeah. I got shot."

"Shot?"

"Twice."

"Oh no!"

"Lost a lot of blood."

"Oh no! How much?"

"A couple of quarts."

"A couple of quarts?!"

"Or pints. Or gallons. I don't know. Whatever they measure blood with, I lost two of 'em. I'll be okay. Don't worry."

I could hear her talking to Brenda. She came back. "Where are you?"

"Uh, I don't know. Let me ask." I found out the hospital's name and told her.

"Oh my God! That's just a quarter of a mile from here."

"Yeah. I was just two blocks away when it happened. I was on time. Really."

"On the corner of Decoro and McBean? That was you?"

"Yeah."

"Oh my God! We heard about it from Tubby and Sue."

"Tubby and Sue? They're the ones taking care of my bike."

She started to cry. "Okay, okay. Don't go anywhere. We're coming down with dinner."

I chuckled. "There's really nowhere for me to go. I mean, you know, I'm hooked up to painkillers, high as a weather ballon, and ready to pass out."

"High as a weather balloon? Never heard that before."

"Me neither."

"Okay. Stay right there. We're coming now." She was still crying. "I'm sorry."

"I'm the one who's sorry, Naomi. I didn't make it."

Brenda and Naomi did come by, but by then I was deep-sleeping. I woke up some time during the night, the only patient in a room with four beds. Brenda had already left for home. Naomi sat right next to my bed, eyes red, looking like she just witnessed the worst disaster in history.

To not make a long story any longer, I'll just say that Naomi – sweet, sweet lady – stayed with me until late the following afternoon. Brenda and James picked us up and took me back to their place where they'd set up a bed for me in Naomi's home.

Now, we've all seen movies where a guy gets beat up or shot a bunch and five minutes later he's knocking boots with some chick. But it's not like that in real life.

Not for me, anyway.

Evidently, all my energy had seeped out along with all that blood. Not that my desire had lessened, what with Naomi walking around in tight jean shorts, tank tops and no bra while taking care of me for two days. Man, what I would have given….

At noon on Saturday, James came over to Naomi's. The meeting with "the boys" was to be in an hour and he wanted to know if I was up for it. I was feeling much better, though my thoughts were more along the lines of having my way with Naomi. Nevertheless, I told James I was good to go.

Naomi and I had only a few minutes so we just loosely held each other. She looked up at me, her eyes wet. "You're coming back, right? So I can keep taking care of you?"

I smiled contentedly and slowly rubbed my hand over her left breast. "I was thinking it was time I took care of you."

She mmm-ed a laugh and tightly held me.

———— ❧ ————

James and I made it to the meeting, which was in a house in Palmdale. All total, there were eight of us: me, James, Tubby (we shook hands and guy-hugged), France (he owned the place), Brian, the mechanic who'd fixed up Naomi's bike, and three others, the names of whom I've forgotten. Bikers all. Everyone but me was somewhat caught up on all the skullduggery Beanie had been up to over the years, but James went over everything anyway.

It turned out that for years Beanie had done things to screw up everyone's lives and livelihoods. (With the exception of me, of course. But then, he didn't even know I existed.) Little things mostly, but when put all together, income had been lost along with friends. Even some family.

But slicing Naomi's brake lines took the proverbial cake. The guy was a righteous piece of work. So the plan to deal with him began.

Of a sudden, we all got quiet, that biker's danger-sense descending on everyone at the same time. Eyes darted back and forth. James said, "Something's not right."

Evidently, Beanie and his buddies had followed James or a few of the other boys to Palmdale because just then, a loud vehicle crash came from the front.

Seconds later, ten or a dozen guys crashed through the front and back doors. Within a few more seconds, they were armed with vases, candleholders, a poker, big books, whatever they could lay their hands on.

Sure, we were somewhat ready but they definitely had the upper hand. And they outnumbered us. Well, bikers are bikers and men are men, so the mayhem commenced. And mayhem it was. Hard, fast and merciless. Sure, my left arm was fifty percent at best, but I was at least able to do some damage.

A half minute into it, the tide began turning to our favor and just after that is when a shot rang out. It took me some moments to realize I'd been hit again. Same shoulder, an inch away from the first bullet wound. This time, the bullet lodged against the skin on the back of my shoulder. Damn, again and again!

James and the rest of the boys doubled their efforts and before a minute ended, Beanie and his buddies (mostly cousins and brothers) were all on the floor moaning and rolling around in blood. James and the boys emptied their wallets to pay for the damage to France's place, then James told all of them to leave. Except for Beanie.

When James got his breath back, he picked up Beanie, held him to the wall with his forearm on his neck, then began pounding him. Over and over and over. Brutal, absolutely brutal. He finally let him fall to the ground then beat his kneecaps and feet to bloody messes with a hammer. So satisfying. More so than watching that guy with the Roadrunner get beaten senseless.

The only real downside was that I'd been shot again. And was losing blood.

Again. Pints, quarts, gallons, whatever. No one called the police, which was fine by me. Instead, a couple of guys helped me to Tubby's pickup then he took me to the hospital.

Later, when the police came to my bed, I told them it was just a random mugging.

I fought back, they shot, story over. They bought it. What choice did they have?

When Naomi found out, she drove straight to Palmdale and stayed with me for two days. She left the morning of the third day in order to get her place ready forme. (She had put everything back the way it had been while I was at the meeting.)

James and Brenda picked me up in the afternoon.

When I got to Naomi's little house, the door was open. Her clothes were gone. Makeup, toiletries, everything. On the coffee table was a note

Lover,

I'm sorry but I have to leave. Beanie's brothers and cousins left a note. They know about you and they've vowed to kill you as long as we're together. I can't let that happen. So I'm moving away to another state.

Gonna change my name, too.

I'm going to miss you so much. I'll never forget our one night. It was the most beautiful ever. You're a great guy. For the first time in my life, I got it right.

Live your life. Be free. Find love. Please, never forget me.

N.

EPILOGUE

It turned out that that guy with the Roadrunner was rich. Tens and tens of millions of dollars rich. He claimed he had been on drugs at the time (probably was) and voluntarily checked into a rehab facility. Of course we all know that the real reason for doing that was to lessen any sentence he would get from trying to kill me.

His high-priced lawyers were eager to settle out of court with me for the same reason. You know, make it look like he was remorseful and taking responsibility. Big scam, really. But I will say this: Ever since then and for the rest of my life, I'll be doing just fine.

Right after the money found its way into my bank account – good gawd was I thrilled! – I quit my job and began riding around the country, living on the road. And I've been doing it ever since. Living the dream every day.

Despite asking them scores of times, James and Brenda claimed to not know where Naomi was or her new name. Though I believed them from the start, I kept asking anyway.

It made sense. I mean, if being in touch with Naomi put my life in danger, then they were in somewhat the same position. Besides, if the three of us didn't know where she was or her new name, then neither Beanie nor his buddies could ever force it out of us.

I never saw Naomi again even though it's been years since I became a denizen of the road. You'd think that time passing would dull the memories and put them out of focus but so far, they're as colorful and as sharp and as can be.

I'd be lying to myself and to you if I said I didn't look for her at every stop sign, every tavern, every campsite, every motel, every town. I keep her note in my pocket. Read it often. Think about her every night before falling asleep.

I'll find her. Someday.

END

MY LITTLE GIRL

I's lucky to get out of there. Real lucky. Can't remember the last time I's that lucky and probably never was. Speaking of luck, I never thought I'd be thanking my lucky stars for vomit. He slipped right on it, fell flat on his ass and I got the hell out. Kinda funny now that I think about it.

Outrun this storm, outrun him, that's how I figure it. Get through it, clear to the other side and I'll be good. No way he can catch me in weather like this, no way. Hell, when I'm on my bike nobody can catch me, period. Tell ya what, though, ain't nothing like looking down the barrel of a 12-gauge to get you to hauling ass.

Hard to believe she's almost eighteen now and I haven't seen her for something like twelve years. Sent her a Christmas present a few times, some birthday presents, too, but most of them Christmases and birthdays I didn't even call. Missed all her soccer and softball games and I think she was into gymnastics for a while but I can't remember.

Missed her junior high school graduation, too, and she even gave a speech at it, forget what they're called. She got real sick twice and I didn't even send her a get well card. And that car accident she got into, didn't send one then, either. She probably even has a boyfriend by now that I don't know the name of.

Damn, it's getting cold. Guess I could run the tank out and get a room. Take a hot shower, warm up the innards with some Southern Comfort. But then, you never know. He does have that 12-gauge and a 12-gauge can do a lot of damage. Kill you, blind you, rip your dick apart, horrible things like that. I should keep riding, get on the other side of this rain, that'd be the safe bet.

I wanted to name her Coraline but Eve wanted Daisy. I tried to insist but Eve wouldn't have it, so we went with Daisy. Face it, I'll stand up to anybody but Eve's one of them people who're so clean of heart and have nothing but good intentions that it's like a bad sin just to disagree with them. Or even have a bad thought about them.

The thing is, Daisy is a damn good name and it fits her better than Coraline ever would have, and I got used to it. Came to like it even.

She used to call me Daddy and tell me she loved me and I can still hear her voice and how sweet and innocent and beautiful it was and how she would wrap them little girl arms around my neck and squeeze as hard as she could and it would just kill me every time because I knew I didn't deserve a little girl who loved me.

Knew it was a bad idea to stop in Kansas City. Felt it in my gut. Hell, every time I've gone to Kansas City was a bad idea. What was with that chick anyways? Going to a bar alone, showing off skin like she did, siding up to me with her hair on my shoulder all soft and smelling nice and pressing them tits on my arm, and giggling and whispering all sorts of I-wanna-fuck stuff. Should've asked about a husband or a boyfriend. Wasn't even that drunk so I don't have an excuse.

Banged it out in the back of her old Toyota, walked back in for a few more beers and all she's talking about is how she wants to go back out and bang it out some more. And then, bang, her fat ugly husband shows up, just like that, like he was waiting on her cue.

What's Eve going to think? Me showing up out of the blue. She has to hate my guts even more now than she did back then. But then, I don't know if she ever did hate me and knowing her she probably didn't. It never was part of her nature to hate anything and that was one of our problems. I deserved to be hated, shit husband that I was. Face it, I'm just shit no matter what I am. Husband, dad, carpenter, roofer, plumber, inmate, whatever. Hell, I ain't even a good drunk and, Lord knows, I work at it.

How'd Mr. Fat Guy end up with a hot chick like her, anyways? Maybe they got some perverted shit going on. She likes fucking strangers and he likes shooting them. Heard about people like that.

44

Whatever it was that was going down, I knew I was fucked when I saw that 12-gauge, but I reckoned it was a righteous comeuppance for all the shit I'd done in my life but mostly for the stuff I never did. Like not being there when Daisy gave that speech. Bet it was a good one, too, about freedom and treating others with respect and love, and working hard for what you believe in and never giving up.

Wish this rain would stop. The wind, too. I'm getting cold, real cold. I should just get a room. Got the money for it – thanks for the roofing work, Frankie! – and why not. Mr. Fat Ugly Husband can't still be following me and chances are he never was.

He probably drives a thirty year old Subaru filled with stale French fries and fried chicken bones and empty potato chip bags and who knows what else. Empty cans of Hormel chili and old Hustler magazines. Dead flies and mud daubers all over. Windows all gray from old dirt that was never washed off.

Probably has a blue mechanic's cloth for a gas cap. Probably needs a valve job, too, and twenty years ago the suspension bottomed out for good from all his weight.

But then there's that 12-gauge. If he is following me, the only way he can catch me is if I stop for the night. Best to keep going.

And what's Eve's lawyer-husband going to think? He's all rich and important and stuff and probably has a mansion on a cliff overlooking the ocean and plays golf with billionaire captains of industry and has the governor's cell phone number.

And I bet he has a couple of yachts and seventeen vintage luxury cars and just as many horses and they're probably the kind with flowing manes and tails that look like they've been washed with expensive French shampoo and ain't never done a lick of decent work.

And they probably have maids and butlers and chefs and groundskeepers and chauffeurs, and a whole gang of horse experts to wash them manes and tails and put expensive French conditioner on them and prance them around so all the good people can clap their gloved hands together and agree to how beautiful they are.

Lightning. I count the seconds before the thunder and it's about five or six miles away. This cold rain ain't letting up but my tires are good so that's at least one thing I don't have to worry about. If it's this cold here, you can be damn sure the Rockies are freezing so I gotta cross them during the day. Gotta be in Southern California late Friday night at the latest so that should work.

Good thing I love riding. If there's one thing I ain't shit at it's riding a motorcycle. But what has that gotten me in life other than getting laid in the back of an old Toyota and a husband waiting with a shotgun?

What made me think going to California was so important that I had to be there anyways? All the things I missed over the years and this comes up and I'm all of a sudden willing to ride over two thousand miles in the rain and risk getting my butt blown off or froze off. Damn it's cold and I'm going to need some gas pretty soon.

I could have taken the truck. Have the heater blasting, listen to some Zac Brown and Dream Theater and what-the-hell-ever I want. Leann Rimes. Now I could listen to Leann forever and never get tired of it.

Could've packed some nice clothes, too. At least the nicest ones I have, which aren't that nice to begin with, but even if I had some nice clothes, really nice like from Macy's or somewhere, they most likely wouldn't be the right clothes to wear to a ballet anyways.

Or is it an opera? Nah, opera's about singing and she's going to be dancing and I'm pretty sure that's ballet. Whatever it is, I hope there's none of that godforsaken singing.

The thing is, that old truck wouldn't have made it over the Rockies. I'd've gotten stuck somewhere and having to look down the barrel of that 12-gauge would have been for nothing.

Taking this old Shovelhead was the right thing to do. It's where I rightly belong anyways and it hasn't given me any problems for years. Of course I did a lot of work on it to get it to what it is – even retooled the frame to my liking and fixed it with an electric starter – and now a brand new Milwaukee-8 can't even begin to compete.

Yeah, the Shovel gives me the best chance of getting there. Hell, it'll still be running when the world runs out of time. What's that line that guy said in that bar down in Galveston that one time? Something something ... till the ocean wears diapers to keep its bottom dry. Something like that.

 Goddamn 18-wheeler flashing his high beams and wants me to pull over. Why can't he pull over and go around? I ain't even in the fast lane. All this thinking and reminiscing must have slowed me down. I'll just throttle back up until he can't see my tail lights no more.

Not looking too bad. Shower, shave, mouthwash, new socks. T-shirt and leather are old but at least they're clean. It's the best I can do and the best I got. I'm a biker, it's important she knows that. But then she already does so there ain't nothing new there. But what'll I say to her? Hey, I'm your dad, remember me?

I'll just sit in the back corner and leave real fast when it's over and not say nothing to nobody. Write her a note later, that'd be best.

I ain't dressed right anyways. They'll probably all be wearing tuxedos and gowns and diamonds and white silk gloves and they'll be driven up to the front doors in limousines by guys in uniforms sitting at attention and guys in uniforms standing at attention will open the doors for them and then they'll be flitting around and eating, I don't know, caviar on imported crackers or something. Yeah, I'll just sit in the back corner in the dark.

One more stoplight and I'm there. Damn I'm nervous. I must be crazy. I should turn around and ride back home right now, stay away from Kansas City, get back to my own living room and listen to some metal. Early Metallica, Master of Puppets, something like that, and get flat-on-my-face drunk.

Okay here it is. I should park in a no-parking space. The regular spaces are probably reserved for Mercedes or BMWs or anything that costs over eighty thousand.

But there's only one no-parking space and it's under a tree and that means bird shit. Don't want no bird shit on the Shovel. Should have washed it before I came but it don't matter, no one will see it anyways.

I look around some more and, sure enough, it's the only no-parking space and it's perfect except for the bird shit. What the hell, the bike's already dirty, I can wash it off tomorrow.

So I'll just walk up these steps and keep looking down and do my best to be invisible. Not talk to anyone and go straight to the will-call window. Remember that I used Cliff's name when I ordered the ticket so nobody would know I was coming. Hope they don't ask for a driver's license. I'll just say I forgot it back at the motel.

The will-call girl's not even sneering at me and she even smiles when she says my name (well, Cliff's name) and tells me to enjoy the ballet. Wasn't expecting civility like that, not for a biker at a ballet.

Hmph, they're selling programs, which is also weird. Thought they only did that at ball games. I'll get one, see if Daisy's name is in it.

"Whatcha riding?"

"Huh?"

"Whatcha riding? You came on your bike, looks like."

The girl's bright and innocent smile stumps me. I frown. "Oh. Yeah, I did. Got an old Shovelhead."

"Awesome! My dad had one, started taking me for rides when I was four. Taught me to kickstart it when I was twelve."

"Really?"

"Yeah, it was great! My brother has a crotch rocket, an R-something, but Harleys are the best."

"That's, uh, cool."

Now that was really weird. A girl selling ballet programs knows about Shovelheads. I should have been nicer, maybe even smiled, talked to her a little. Oh well, too late now. Now it's time to find that dark corner but I need a drink first. I look all around and all there is to drink is water. Not even any beer. What kind of public event don't even sell beer?

Hell, I'll just slip into this bathroom, hide in a stall, pull out my flask and throw down a few shots. Damn, Southern Comfort always tastes better than I remember.

Okay, I'll just walk down this dark hallway to the theater and keep looking at my feet and keep being invisible and open this door and sneak into the back corner and, damn!, this place is lit up like I'm right in front of one of them highway patrol spotlights! Somebody's gonna see me for sure.

Daisy's getting ready to dance, probably stretching and stuff, so it'll probably be Eve or her rich lawyer-husband and they'll want me to leave and I will because I don't fit in and I don't want to cause no trouble for Daisy. I can't let them see me so I'll bury my head in this program and read it until they turn the lights off.

So, it's a ballet called Thumbelina. I think I read that story once. Maybe not. Written by some guy from Iceland or something like that. Portugal, Denmark, Tasmania, hell I don't know where he was from. Don't matter, he's probably dead by now.

Cast of Characters. Where's her name? Daisy, Daisy … there it is, Daisy Dawn Ramsdell. Woah. My last name, not her stepfather's. She still remembers me, ain't that something? Another thing I wasn't expecting.

Wait. She's going to be the Swallow? That's a fucking bird for crissakes. Daisy should be Thumbelina, not some fucking feathered freak. If the girl playing Thumbelina is younger than Daisy, I'm going to … okay okay, hold on a minute, that's your temper and the Southern Comfort talking and they're making you get all riled up for nothing. I mean, her name is bigger than almost everyone else's so that's something.

Hmm. Four pages of bios and photos. That Thumbelina gal is definitely older, in her twenties, so I guess Daisy is working her way up. Maybe next year or the year after she'll be Thumbelina, that'd be good. But where's her picture? It's got to be here somewhere, right? Damn, I can't even recognize my own daughter.

There it is. The Swallow: Daisy Dawn Ramsdell. I can't believe that's her. Lord she's beautiful, a beautiful young woman. The smile, the light in her eyes, the angle of her head, her hair all natural and waving down across one cheek like an angel's kiss.

"Excuse me, are these seats taken?"

"Uh, no, I mean I don't know, I mean, yeah you can sit there I guess. This place is filling up fast."

"My name's Margie and this is Francine. You don't mind sitting next to two old ladies, do you?"

"Not at all, if you don't mind sitting next to a biker."

"Oh I love motorcycles." She and Francine do their best to arrange their purses and get comfortable. "My first husband rode an old hardtail when we were dating and I told him I wouldn't marry him until he got a bike with a comfortable seat for me. He went right out and traded it for an old Hydra Glide with a back seat, rode straight over to my house and asked me to marry him."

"Is that right?"

"It is! The first weekend we rode up the Pacific Coast Highway and it was the most glorious feeling. The wind and the sky and the freedom. It felt like we'd just escaped from jail. We stopped at every place we could find where no one could see us and … oh you know."

"Yeah. I mean, I can imagine."

"Imagine? Don't try to fool me." She gave me a mischievous smile. "A big hunk like you must have hot babes riding bitch all the time."

"Well, I, uh…"

"It's okay. Francine and I may be old but we've been around. So, are you a big fan of ballet?"

"It's my first time."

"Really? Oh, you'll love it! Our favorite is the scene with the Swallow. It's so beautiful and it always makes us cry. It's our favorite music, too, isn't it, Francine?"

Francine looks around Margie and nods and smiles and says, "There's a new girl dancing it this year. Hope she can do it as well as the last one."

"I'm sure she will."

———∿———

So the first act is over and I didn't see a swallow or Daisy but just like Margie said, I did like it, which is strange because I never thought I would enjoy a ballet. Or ever go to one. Hell, I can count on one hand the times I ever even thought about ballet.

I kept thinking that that Thumbelina gal sure is going through some tough times, like all of us have at one time or another, or almost all the time for some of us. I feel sorry for her. I want her to find her way back home to her Mom and find the Prince and have nothing bad ever happen to her again.

The music is like something I've never heard. I mean, it's beautiful and all, except for that Witch stuff and the Beetle part, that was some weird shit, but whoever did it is no pop rocker, I can tell you that. How can anybody even think of music like that? All them instruments that nobody knows the names of. Must be some old guy from some place in Europe and he's probably dead like Hans Christian Anderson and probably has three names, too, that are weird and impossible to spell.

Damn, there's Eve walking out to the lobby. If I don't straight look at her she won't look at me, that's the way it works, right? Like when you're out hunting deer you don't look right at them because if you do they can feel you looking at them and then they'll run off, so you look a little to either side of them. Works like that with people, too; look to the side of them a little and they'll never notice you.

She looks terrific, still has all them soft curves like when we were together. And she looks happy, contented, and so does her lawyer-husband. They look good together. Maybe I did something right by letting her go.

But that's bullshit. I didn't let her go, I left her, bastard that I am. But she's better off without me. Daisy, too. Maybe I'm better off, too, because now I don't have all the guilt I would have had if I'd stuck around and made their lives miserable.

Okay, the place is almost empty now and no one's looking over, I'm just gonna slip this flask out of my pocket and … damn, I love this stuff. Gets me buzzed and buzzed good.

50

Okay, so here's the second act. Now, I know I'm a little drunk, or a lot, I don't know, but if I don't see Daisy real soon I'm going to complain to somebody. The question is who. That Hans Christian Anderson guy is already dead so who is there to talk to?

I'm listening and watching and now I'm feeling really sorry for Thumbelina. I feel like going up there and taking her hand and letting her partake of my flask and getting her to tell me all about her woes and then help her find her Mom and the Prince.

The Prince seems like an okay guy because he's all forlorn, too, because he can't find Thumbelina. Somebody needs to help these people, goddammit, they're in love!

Thumbelina keeps walking and looking around and now she meets a Mouse. I don't trust that Mouse, something about her ain't right and, sure enough, there she is making Thumbelina scrub the floors and stuff, turning her into a kind of slave.

And now she's being hunted by a big spider? What the fuck! Can this poor girl ever get a break?

I need another drink. I wonder if I take my flask out would I get in trouble and get kicked out. Wouldn't be the first time I've been kicked out of a place but if I did get kicked out, I'd never get to see Daisy dance. But then, Margie and Francine are the only ones who'd see me and Margie did say they've been around so maybe they'd understand and not say nothing. I don't know. It feels risky.

Fuck it, I need a drink. Nice long swallow. Damn that's smooth. And now Margie's elbowing me and wants some so I pass her the flask and she takes a hit and passes it to Francine. Hope there'll be some left when I get it back. Now all three of us are buzzing. Wonder if they're as worried about Thumbelina as me.

Good. Thumbelina got away from that spider. And now who does she run into instead of the Prince? Some goddam ugly Rodent who thinks he's God's gift to women because he's rich. Now I'm pissed. I mean, I hate guys like that. And now he's forcing her to dance with him. That's just not right. I'm starting to see red.

I wonder what would happen if I just went up there and popped him in his ugly rodent nose a couple or three times. Damn, I need to settle down here, have another few swigs from the flask. Margie and

Francine probably need another hit or two. I mean, this is tough to watch.

Oh good, Thumbelina finally got away from the Rodent and now he and the Mouse are walking away and, shit! What the fuck!

The Swallow, my little girl, is on the ground, all hurt and everything, maybe even dying or dead! What kind of fucked up ballet shit is this! What demented mind made my little girl be all injured and dying or dead?

And now the Rodent shoves her out of his way with his foot? He kicks my little girl? Are you fucking kidding me? I ain't taking this no more, he's in for it. He's going down and going down hard. I try to get up but Margie holds me back. She's strong, too, for an elderly lady. Must be the Southern Comfort.

Wait. Thumbelina is going over to her. She's helping Daisy get better and now she's getting up. It looks like my little girl is going to be okay. Now she's starting to dance. And she keeps dancing and dancing and turning and leaping and spinning and moving around all effortless-like, like magnolias waving in a summer breeze.

I'm crying. Can't help it and don't care. That's my little girl up there and it's the most beautiful, sweetest, most wonderful thing I've ever seen. Margie puts her hand on my arm and I can tell she's crying, too. So is Francine.

Why am I still here? I sure don't belong in a crowd like this. I look around and it's the likes of which I've never seen before. People laughing and hugging and holding bunches of flowers and kids running around playing tag and no one's yelling or mad or threatening to hit each other. I might have to drain my flask just to deal with all this happy goodness.

I should just go, get my ass out of here and not embarrass myself or anyone else.

"John?"

Shit. Lawyer-husband. Knew I should have left. "Hey."

"Good Lord! You rode all the way from Kentucky just to see Daisy dance? That's wonderful!"

"Yeah, I guess I did." He's shaking my hand like he's happy I'm here and, dammit, I start to believe he is.

"Does she know you're here?"

"Nah, I didn't say nothing. Figured she probably wouldn't want to see me. Eve, too."

"Oh no, they're going to love this! Hold on, stay right here." Shit, he's going to get Eve. Guess I can't leave now.

"John?"

I turn around and it's Eve and she's as beautiful as I remember and she still has that velvety energy all around her, like it flows out of her and into the air for everyone else to breathe. She stops and looks at me like she's seeing a ghost. "Oh goodness, it *is* you!" She comes over and hugs me real long and hard and kisses me on the cheek a bunch and I don't know why. "I'm so glad you came. Have you seen Daisy yet?"

"Nah, she don't know I'm here. I didn't want to upset her."

"Upset her? Oh John, you silly man, she's going to love that you're here. She won't be out for a few minutes. Let's go over there and talk." She leads me to a low brick wall and we sit. "How are you, John?"

"Pretty good, I guess. Working some, enough to get by. Riding a lot. How 'bout you?"

We get each other caught up on the few goings-on we didn't know about and I gotta say it's real nice talking to her after all these years. She's a damn good woman.

It takes a while but I finally get the courage to ask her what she told Daisy about me. She leans in close, puts her hand on my arm and looks me in the eye. "I told her you loved her and always would, that you were a good man and always would be. I told her that some people have a wanderlust inside of them that never goes away and if people love them, they will let them go. It was hard on her, on me, too, but we got through it. Your letters and emails helped a lot."

"I never wrote much."

"Oh, you wrote a lot, John."

"I did?"

"Yes. Daisy still has every letter and a printout of every email. They fill up a bunch of bankers boxes in the garage and all the stuffed animals you sent practically fill up her bedroom. And the cards you sent when she was sick, and she swears the big one you sent with the huge teddy bear when she got into that car accident is what got her through all her physical therapy."

"Really? I don't remember any of that."

"I'm not surprised, you could never remember anything."

"Got that right."

"How many times did you forget to take your wallet with you?"

"'Bout three or four times a week." We laugh and it's a good laugh, relaxed and easy.

"She looks up to you. Brags about you."

"She does?"

"Oh yes. A few years ago, she had a school assignment to write an essay on freedom. It was all about you."

"Really?"

"It was after that that she wanted to change her last name back to Ramsdell. Max took her downtown himself and helped her get through the whole process."

"Max is your husband?"

She smiles that sweet smile I remember. "Yes."

"He did that? He didn't get pissed or nothing?"

"Max? Oh no. He loves Daisy, helped raise her like she was his own, but he knows you're the dad. She calls him 'Max' but you're 'Daddy', or 'Dad' now that she's a teenager, and he never tried to get her to do otherwise."

My eyes get all watery and I'm starting to cry again when I see Daisy. People are going up to her and shaking her hand and giving her flowers and hugging her and saying congratulations and taking pictures with her. I can't move, don't want to move. I don't want to do nothing but sit here and look at my grown up little girl.

Eve is standing now and tugging on my arm. "Come on, John." We walk over and then Daisy sees me. Her eyes get real big and her mouth is slightly open. Then she runs up to me and wraps her arms around my neck and squeezes real hard, just like she did twelve years ago, and I can't believe how good it feels.

"Daddy! You're here!"

"Yeah."

"I can't believe it!"

"I can't either, I guess. You looked real pretty up there."

She hugs me again. "Thanks! And thank you so much for coming."

"Wouldn't miss it. You were real pretty."

"You already said that, silly."

"I know. I wanted to say something else but that's all I could think of."

"Oh, I'm so glad you came."

54

"I'm glad I came, too, Daisy." And again she wraps them arms around my neck and squeezes real hard.

Daisy introduces me to some of the other dancers and makes me get into pictures with them. I tell the Thumbelina gal that I'm sorry she had to go through all the bad things she did. I tell Thumbelina's Mom that I'm real happy she got reunited with her daughter. I tell the Prince that he's a good man for not giving up on finding Thumbelina and I compliment the Fairy King and Queen on looking past differences of species and letting Thumbelina marry the Prince.

The Rodent is holding his two-year-old daughter and standing next to his wife and I don't know what to think about it. If he's married and has a daughter, why was he hitting on Thumbelina? I try to be diplomatic so as not to upset his daughter so I tell him I'm happy Margie stopped me from busting his nose wide open. At first, they look at me like I'm nuts but then they laugh and say thank you and then we pose for more pictures.

Daisy, Eve and Max insist I go to the wrap party but I don't know what that is so they explain it to me. I follow them there and Daisy's in the back seat of their car smiling at me through the back window the whole time. I wave and she waves. I pretend like I'm falling down and she laughs. I play nighttime-daytime with her, covering my eyes then uncovering them and opening them real big like I did when she was a toddler, and every time she acts surprised and giggles just like she did back then.

When we get there, Daisy stays by my side and introduces me to everyone I didn't meet before, even to a lady called the artistic director and choreographer. I don't know what a choreographer is but she looks like she used to be a damn fine ballet dancer herself.

After a while, I'm getting thirsty and thinking I could use a beer and right when I think that, Daisy looks at me and says, "Want me to get you a beer?" I say I do and while she's gone I'm thinking I'm a little hungry, too, and when she comes back she carrying a cold Modelo Negra and a piece of boysenberry pie. Man, am I feeling fine.

Max and Eve come up to me and Max says that he and Eve and some of their friends are going for a three day, two night ride starting tomorrow and they want me to come along. He says that one couple can't make it so I can use their motel reservations and because I'm

Daisy's dad they'd like it to be a gift and they don't want me to pay them back, which is real nice.

I'm figuring that because Max and his friends are rich they're probably either a bunch of newbies or weekend posers and every time I've ridden with people like that, I get frustrated and sometimes pissed off. But he's been real decent to me and did a damn sight better job of being a father than I could have, so I say okay.

Then Eve says why don't I let Daisy ride on the back and I think that's a fine idea and so does Daisy.

———————

Early the next morning I get to Eve and Max's house and it's a real nice one and pretty big but not the mansion I thought it'd be. There aren't no luxury cars or fancy horses or maids or butlers or servants. I can see the ocean from their back yard but it's a good three or four blocks away. Max rides a newer Electra Glide and there are two other Harleys, three Beemers, two Japanese tourers, and a Goldwing. All the guys come over to admire my Shovelhead and it makes me proud.

We take off and the traffic on the freeway is slow and thick. Max, who's leading, splits lanes and we all follow. At first I'm nervous because it's against the law in all the places I've lived in for the last twelve years but I guess in California it's still okay. We even pass a cop and he just looks at us and smiles a little. Sometimes the traffic opens up and Max takes off accordingly and it seems like he knows what he's doing.

We spend the night at a sort of upscale log cabin motel in Wrightwood, which is at the east end of Angeles Crest, which I remember to be a world class canyon, all sixty miles of it. Because Daisy's with us I keep my drinking to a minimum and don't mind it much.

My riding partners tell me that Angeles Forest ain't nearly as lush as it was before the Station Fire but that it's nice to see Mother Nature fighting her way back. They also tell me that instead of repaving the Crest like it should have been done, the yahoo transportation bigwigs in Sacramento decided that since the traffic is nothing but skiers and sightseers and bikers, there's not much commercial value to the route so chip sealing it would be good enough because it's cheap.

Chipseal leads to pot holes which they fill up with whatever may or may not do the job but there are, as yet, not very many pot holes and no deep ones. Maybe these people are a step above weekenders, who knows. Guess I'll find out tomorrow.

We get up early and head on over to the Grizzly Cafe. Our waitress is a real pretty blond but for some reason I don't come on to her. It's an odd way for me to act but I gotta say it's nice, comfortable even, to just be pleasant with a pretty lady without having to figure out what to say or do to get her in the sack.

When we take off, the sky is pure blue and the clouds are white with a few gray ones tucked in here and there. The air is a little cold, brisk as one of the ladies calls it, but only cold or brisk enough to let you know that it's about as clean as air can get in Southern California.

Max is still leading and he rides pretty damn good. Respectable speed, avoids sand and gravel, doesn't overuse his brakes and I admire that. He leans good in the corners and Eve leans right with him and, man, is that a pretty sight: two people riding like one. Daisy is a knowledgeable passenger, too, and I quickly get to the point where I don't have to worry about her.

Our speed is relaxing but not boring and everyone seems comfortable with it. The only thing is that they like to point out road hazards with their left hands and right feet and to me that's always been annoying because if you need someone else to point out road hazards for you, you're just not paying attention, and I always pay attention to the road even when I'm drunk. Despite that, these are good people and that's what I start thinking about.

I think about the fact that I ain't seen no one drink too much or throw a punch or even get pissed off a little. None of the guys have complained to or about their lady and vice versa and I don't know what to make of it.

Maybe they're that one-in-a-million group of friends that always gets along, I don't know. I do know that I'm starting to like it. Makes me feel like there's no need to keep my guard up or have to defend myself or get into all that bravado shit.

Like they told me the night before, there are a lot dead trees, all charred black and reaching up like they died in agony in that Station Fire. And a lot of places where there ain't no plant life at all. But like they said, Mother Nature has made sure that new growth is never far away and I begin to think that maybe life is like that. That you can go through hell and end up in a desolate place that's unforgiving and harsh but the opposite is just "over there" within reach.

We stop at Newcomb's Ranch for a cold drink but not for food because, according to Max, it takes forever to get a meal and we have a long ways to go. A couple of the guys and gals get a beer but Daisy wants a lemonade so that's what I get, too.

Our destination for the day is the coast and the idea is to get there in time to watch the sun set over the Pacific Ocean. That sounds like a fine idea to me, and from the conversation, I come to believe that trying to determine how beautiful a sunset will be by watching the clouds is a common habit of bikers.

Once we're back outside, the only solo rider, Mateo, who's a tad older than Daisy, comes up to me and says that everyone lets him take off by himself sometimes and that's exactly what he's going to do for the last half of the Crest, which is the curviest, and he wants to know if I'll join him.

Daisy tells me that he rode Moto 3 for a year and last year placed sixth in Moto 2 and I notice there's a thing, a connection, between the two. Mateo looks at me square like he's saying he's keeping his distance until she turns eighteen and I look back as if I'm saying that's a good idea.

I ask Mateo about his riding and he lets me know he's damn good, but he does it in a matter-of-fact way, no boasting. I like that. He also tells me he has a spot set aside in his home for the MotoGP championship trophy but he has a long ways to go before he can challenge Rossi and Marquez.

He asks again if I want to ride the last half of the Crest with him. I look at his padded and armored riding gear and at my jeans, vest and fingerless gloves. I look at his full faced helmet and at my skullcap. I look at his beefed-up Beemer with its 150 horsepower and at my forty year old Shovelhead and tell him why the hell not.

Before we take off, he says he wants me to lead. I know he's saying that because he wants to check me out, see what kind of rider I am and all, but that's okay. I know how to take a canyon. Daisy and I head off down that first straightaway at a moderate speed, even a little slow and just before the first curve, I lean back and tell Daisy to hold on and hold on tight and she does.

Then we hit it. Every turn, every twisty, every s-curve like they were waiting to be chewed up and spit out. Daisy shrieks a couple of times and I pat her knee to let her know we're okay. Mateo's close but not too close and I'm impressed at how he keeps the exact same distance all the time.

I twist the throttle harder and harder, lean more and more, even scoot my butt to the inside of the seat, and still he's right there. We pass by guys on sport bikes and they're shocked and a few are pissed and feel challenged but there's nothing they can do about it.

The sound of the Shovel's V-twin is bellowing off the canyon walls like they're the walls of Jericho and it's beautiful. Explosions of testosterone ripping the air apart.

Up ahead is a big U-turn covered with sand and gravel but instead of slowing down, I throttle into it and drift through it with Daisy screaming as loud as the Shovel, and the sand splays against the mountainside like a giant wave crashing into Gibraltar.

I look in my rear view mirror and, sure enough, Mateo is still right there. The kid is damn good. I straighten up and slam the next curve and the next and the next and the next and my senses are on fire and every sinew and muscle and bone, every gear and valve lift and exhaust push are howling in concert, redlining for the gods of speed.

Toward the bottom, as we come into some neighborhoods, we slow down and after we make a broad left turn we pull over to the side, about a half-mile from the 210 Freeway. Daisy jumps off, gets into my face and screams, "That was awesome!" and gives me a hug that just about breaks my neck. Mateo runs over and says, "I love they way you ride canyons!" and gives me a bear hug that just about breaks my back. Damn, I'm feeling as fine as I've ever felt.

⁓

After Max and Eve and their friends catch up to us, we head west on the 210 Freeway then north on Interstate 5. We pull into a gas station at the southern end of Frazier Park and top off our tanks. Max then leads us to Lockwood Valley Road and it's here that I begin thinking about my friends back home.

At first I compare them to my present company and wonder why they're always arguing and complaining and how nothing's ever right for them. Except for Cliff and Pascal, of course. They've been together forever, since they started grammar school, and they never get on each other's ass.

And Bob and Linda. They're always cool except for that one six month stretch, but that was when Bob's dad and Linda's mom were dying and Bob lost his job and their house got broken into. But even then, now that I think about it, they were just mad, not mad at each other. And we all helped them out with money and food, and they stayed together through all that.

And Paul and Patsy. Something's always going wrong with them, sure, but somehow they're always there when you need them. And they're always there for each other, too, especially when they get sick and they get sick a lot.

And my buddies Frankie, Cash, Trap and Newt. Shit man, them guys will drink with you for days while you're getting over the fact that your girlfriend's been banging the new bartender in town. Except for Newt. He'll pass out after just two beers or a shot of whiskey and there's no sense to it, being that he weighs almost four hundred pounds.

Our speed is still a good one and it seems like everybody's even more relaxed than we were yesterday. Especially compared to the way Mateo and I hit the Crest. Except for when we crossed that muddy stream that was flowing over the road. But no one went down or even wavered.

The air is clean and every now and then it's filled with the smell of sage. There are real pretty views over to the right and with Daisy on the back, it couldn't be better. Hell, I don't know what's going on but when we passed that sign for the Reyes Cantina, I didn't even get an itch for a beer.

Lockwood Valley Road deadends at Highway 33 where we pull into a turnout to stretch our legs. Max says we're making good time and if we don't dilly-dally we'll be able to get a quick bite to eat at the Deer Lodge in Meiner's Oaks, which is right next to Ojai, and still make it to the coast to see that sunset. I look at the clouds and I'm thinking it's going to be a gorgeous one.

The 33 is a killer route and we keep going at a good pace, rolling past all sorts of killer views and I get back to thinking about my friends in Kentucky. I take a good long look at all the bickering and unhappiness and it's a surprise to realize that there just ain't that much of it. And the more I look at it, the more I come to believe that everyone back there gets along just as well as Eve and Max and their friends.

I wonder why I always thought it was otherwise and then I remember something I read once. Or maybe I heard or saw in a movie, I don't know. When you look at other people, what you're really looking at is yourself, that you actually judge others by how you think you yourself should be judged. I don't know if that's true, but if it is then I'm the one with the anger, I'm the one unsettled and spreading strife. Like

Cliff once told me. "Shit John, you get into more wranglings than everybody else I know put together."

He's right. And despite that, my friends have stuck by me and helped me whenever I needed it and I've needed it a lot. And I begin to think that maybe my life ain't as fucked up as I thought it was.

———

We get to the Deer Lodge and each order a burger or a salad. Max tells the waitress we need to get to the coast in time to see the sunset and she's real quick about bringing our food. I notice everyone tips her real well so that's what I do, too.

We ride through Ojai then follow Highway 150 west, which is a damn pretty route. When we ride by houses close to the road, Max slows down like he should, and when we go by empty fields he speeds up a good bit. It's like we're racing the sun just like I did that storm a few days ago.

I look around and see some cows and a few horses grazing. Avocado and persimmon and walnut trees, and a huddle of palm trees that look like they belong in Hawaii or some place.

Agave plants and the red buds of holly and pyracantha, and jasmine flowers that look like little baby hands in white gloves with the fingers spread out wide. When we pass through a stretch filled with the smell of lilacs, both me and Daisy breathe in real deep.

There are kids playing in a small, blow-up plastic swimming pool and a young man washing his old Camaro. A woman in a broad brimmed hat trims her rose bushes while her husband fixes the door of their motorhome.

Again I take in a deep breath and the cooling air makes me think about the just-might-be fact that I thought my life was shit only because I thought that's what I deserved. And the reason I thought I deserved a shit life was because of all the things I failed to do.

But when I think of all them letters and emails and cards and stuffed animals I sent Daisy, I guess I did do some good things, that I did come through now and then.

And I think that, sure, my friends have helped me a lot but I've helped them out of a lot of jams, too. Maybe, just maybe, I've been pushing myself down all these years because I figured I was a shit person when I wasn't. I ain't perfect, not by a long shot, but still, maybe I ain't the useless scum I've been thinking I was.

Oh hell, I don't know, I ain't good at all this introspection shit.

But there are some things I do know. I know that I'm riding my Shovelhead, a bike that sends a rumble up through my bones telling me I'm alive and I'm here and I make a difference. I know that over to my left is a lake, Lake Casitas I think, and it stretches out in the afternoon light like an enormous hand of burning sapphire and when I look at the clouds in the distance and the clouds reflected in its waters, I can see the whole sky and I am part of it. I know that, just like the sky, the heart is never empty and that it always courses through us the warm blood of family and friendship.

I know that when I come home from a three month ride, tired and hungry and broke, my friends will feed me and find work for me and I'll appreciate it and they'll appreciate me for doing a good job. I know that when you pull someone up from the bottom, your hands will get dirty but it's okay because there'll come a time when you'll need some pulling up yourself.

I know that Eve and Max and countless other mothers and fathers will always take care of those entrusted to them. And I know that behind me, right now, is a young woman holding me like a little girl who doesn't want to let go of her Daddy.

We park in the graveled parking area of Carpenteria Bluffs, wend our way single-file along a path through the bushes, over some railroad tracks, and to the edge of some cliffs where, down below, small waves are putting wrinkles of foam onto a narrow strip of sand. We sit and watch the sun slowly color the clouds yellow and orange and purple.

I look at Daisy, her eyelashes flicking down and up with elegance, her eyes like crystals that are alive, her mouth in a pose of wonder. She gently holds onto my arm, her hair on my shoulder soft and cool. She looks up at me and smiles. "I love you, Daddy."

END

THE NETTLES GANG

What are they eating?"

"Nettles."

I thought about that. Aren't nettles those little green plants with invisible thorns that hurt like hell for days? I remembered one morning some years before. I was sitting on my back porch wearing nothing but a bathrobe and enjoying my first cup of coffee for the day.

For some reason, I decided to pull some weeds, so I walked to the back fence, knelt down, then did just that. A minute or so later, I scraped my, um, manhood and two sacks of future babies across a nettles plant. Agony! I couldn't cross my legs for three days.

I looked at the nettles-eaters with a bit of awe. "Nettles?"

"Yeah. It's a contest."

"A contest?"

"Yeah. See who can eat the most in five minutes."

I continued looking at the six men who were chowing down like they had been starving their whole lives and it was the first time they'd tasted a chocolate donut. My eyebrows scrunched. "Is that smart?"

"Well, they ain't poison so at least it ain't totally stupid."

I was in a park in a place called Friendship. It was a sort of celebratory gathering, what with kids running around and dogs barking and wagging their tails, and about sixty adults standing around whooping and clapping while six grown men stuffed thorn-laden plants into their mouths. I'd never seen anything like it. But hey, it was my first time in Arkansas and who knows what passes for normal around here.

It was springtime going on summer and the last week of getting there included some of the most pleasant riding any biker could ever hope for. Sure it rained a bunch but evidently here in the South, rain means warm weather, which is totally opposite of Western Washington, which is where I hail from.

My stuff was packed up such that nothing ever got wet, except for me and the bike and the outside of the bags, and deciding on the best clothes for the day was easy peasy. (Well, easy peasy once I got genned in to the warm rain.)

It was the first long trip with my new Road Glide. Well, new to me, anyway. It was nine years old, clean inside and out, and had only 14,600 miles when I bought it nine months before. The brakes were fresh, the tranny was locked in, and the new tires had only a thousand or so miles on them, so everything was as good as good can get.

A ball rolled against the legs of the lady I'd been talking with. She picked it up and threw it back to a young girl. "Thanks, Clearly!"

So the lady's name was Clearly – an odd name but, like I said, who knows what passes for normal in Arkansas – and it turned out that she was married to the eventual winner of the nettles eating contest. When he came over to get a victory kiss, she pushed him away and said, "Wash yer mouth out, Raul. Don't want none of them nettles on my lips."

Raul was a good six inches over six feet tall with a barrel-chest and thick arms covered with tattoos. He had short hair and a perfectly trimmed, around-the-face black beard that had a few gray hairs in it. He smiled a big and gleaming smile. (Well, except for some green nettles plant particles between his teeth.) "I do love you, Baby."

"I love you, too, Darling. Now you go on and wash that mouth out."

The others in the contest and their ladies came over. One of them said, "You stop feeding him for a week, Clearly? He was chowing down like a starving horse on sweet red apples. First time he's ever won."

"Nah, didn't do nothing like that. He's just focused, I guess."

I started thinking about nettles again. How could anyone actually eat them? I mean, geez, these guys must have titanium stomachs.

One of the nettles-eaters nodded my way then asked Clearly, "Who's yer friend?"

"Don't know." She looked at me. "What's yer name anyways?"

"Jerry."

"Well shit," the Nettles-Eater said, "Pleased to meet ya. Name's Jerry, too. This here's my lady, June."

We shook hands and my own hand immediately began burning from the nettles that covered his. The other four also introduced their ladies and themselves and shook my hand. At the end of it, it felt like I was holding burning coals. But those five guys? They acted as if they wore down mittens.

Clearly's husband came back, gave her a big kiss, then looked at me and said, "That yer Road Glide, stranger?"

Clearly broke in. "His name's Jerry."

"Shit. We got another Jerry? Always figured the one we had was one too many."

Jerry-the-Nettles-Eater said, "Go jump headfirst in a dried up lake, Raul."

Everyone, including Raul, laughed. Raul looked at me again. "Where ya from?"

"Washington."

"D.C. or the state?"

"The state."

His eyes opened wide. "You ride all the way from there?"

"I did."

"Alone?"

"Yep."

He looked me down and up. "Well sheeit! Ain't that something! You must be one helluva demon on that thing."

"Not really. I take it slow a lot."

"Even so, I bet yer still better than that Jerry over there."

Jerry-the-Nettles-Eater said, "Make that a lake full of copperheads." Everyone laughed again.

Without any kind of invitation, I walked with them to the tables for lunch. As friendly as they were, it felt like the right and natural thing to do. On the one hand, the camaraderie was welcoming, what with everyone smiling and joking around and such. All in all, they seemed like fine folks and it wasn't long before I felt like one of them.

On the other hand, I couldn't get it out of my thoughts that these guys actually eat nettles. What else do they do? Chase down wild hogs and eat them alive?

The partying lasted through an early lunch, which consisted of three roasted pigs, heads and all, cornbread, beans, potato and macaroni salads, beer, homemade moonshine, and a big table covered with desserts. If there were any vegetables, they were hidden someplace where I never looked.

Once everyone had their fill, Raul looked at me for a some moments as if he was measuring me up, like he had me in mind for some sort of task. He walked over, sat next to me, pulled out a map, an actual paper map, then pointed to Ouachita Lake. "We're gonna be riding there in a bit. You're welcome to join us."

I looked at the map and said, "Oh-uh-CHEETA Lake?"

Everyone laughed. Clearly said, "Boy, you really ain't from around here, are ya?"

With a big smile, Raul clued me in. "It's called WASH-uh-taw. About an hour and a half ride. There's a nice little place there called Marilyn's."

Now, I've always prided myself on my good manners and willingness to join in with others so this was an invitation I couldn't really refuse. But in the back of my mind, I was still thinking about those nettles and the fact that that day was a run-of-the-mill Sunday. What do these guys do on holidays? Eat rusted two-penny nails?

———✕———

Everyone but me rode two-up. Jerry was the Road Captain so he and June took the lead. Raul was evidently the most experienced because he and Clearly brought up the rear. My place was right in front of them.

The roads were in okay to pretty good shape, but man, the areas we rode through were pure Americana. Well-kept farms fronted by painted rail fences, mom-and-pop shops here and there, campgrounds nestled among low hills, lots of ponds.

The trees and bushes became more and more abundant as we entered the Ouachita National Forest, and riding through them felt like shaking hands with all your friends.

We'd just turned a blind corner when we came to a fellow standing in the middle of the road pointing a shotgun at us. We stopped. Nobody reacted. Except for me. It'd been a good ten years since I'd been a Military Policeman in the Marines and anyone had pointed a gun at me, so for a good minute I was shaking like one of those massage chairs at a broken-down car wash.

But the nettles-eaters and their ladies? To tell you the truth, they all looked positively bored. Raul, with Clearly still sitting behind him, rode to the front, pushed down the kickstand, then climbed off.

The man with the shotgun said, "Y'alls on private property." Raul casually walked toward him with his head down. "Don't you come no closer." Raul kept walking. "I'm warning ya." Raul kept walking. The man pointed the gun right at Raul's face. "I'm telling ya. I'll shoot!"

Raul stopped a half foot in front of the barrel then looked around at the trees and the sky like he was out for a lazy stroll, deciding whether to keep going or head on home. He finally looked at the shotgun-wielding man and said, "Put the damn shotgun down, Earl. You ain't shooting nobody today."

Earl relaxed a bit "Just protecting what's mine. This here's private property."

"It ain't private property, Earl. It's a public road maintained by the Arkansas Department of Transportation."

Earl's eyes darted back and forth. "Cuts right through my land."

"This road don't cut through nothing. Alls you got is two acres a mile up that dirt road back over there." Raul put his hands on his hips and sympathetically looked at Earl some moments. "How's the old lady? Kids?"

"What do you care?"

"Just making conversation."

At first glance, Earl seemed to be in his sixties but on closer inspection was most likely in his late thirties or early forties. Skinny as a tetherball pole, long and scraggly beard, wild hair sticking out every which way; old pants worn to a shine, a shirt that looked like it was once a sack of flour, shoes that had been stitched together who knows how many times. His shotgun now drooped down pointing at the road along with his head.

Raul said, "Come on hard times again?" Earl gently kicked at the asphalt. Raul looked back at us then at Earl again. "Okay, this is what we're gonna do. We'll each give you twenty bucks…"

Earl flashed at Raul and barked with mountain pride. "I don't need no charity!"

"It ain't charity, Earl. We be paying for the right to pass this here road." Earl, with a suspicious look, listened intently. "But just to be clear, now, twenty bucks gives each of us passage up the road *and* back down. Deal?"

Earl shrugged his shoulders. "I guess."

Raul walked back to the group, got a twenty-dollar bill from each of us, then walked back to Earl. "Here's 260 bucks. Go buy some food."

Earl put the bills in his shirt pocket. "Cain't."

"Why?"

"Pickup's got no more than a spoonful of gas in it."

Raul took a long sigh then looked back at Jerry, who climbed off his bike then unfastened a full, one gallon gas can from the back of it. He walked over to Earl then handed it to him.

Raul said, "Okay, the gallon will get ya to a gas station." He got out his wallet again then pulled out another twenty-dollar bill. "Here's another twenty for gas. Just leave the can alongside the road and we'll get it when we come back."

Earl, looking back down, took the twenty. "Thank you, Raul." He paused and looked up. "I wasn't gonna shoot ya, ya know."

"I know that, Earl, I know that. Now you just go on and take care of yer family."

———— ∿ ————

We took off. The trees and bushes and green hills were comforting as was the warm air and it's during times like that, that I, along with most any biker, begin to reflect. And that scene I just witnessed captured all of my attention.

I mean, think about it: A wild mountain man stops us with a shotgun and nobody reacts, not a nervous soul among us, except for me, that is. And Raul talks to him like they're chatting over a morning cup of coffee.

Then I started thinking that, man, these guys eat nettles and who knows what else, poisonous spiders probably, yet they have no problem showing monetary compassion to a guy who looked like he was going to shoot us. I had no idea what was going on but I did realize that those Arkansas folks were a breed the likes of which I'd never before come across.

It wasn't long before we got to Marilyn's RV Park and Old Country Store, the proprietors being Marilyn herself and her father, Mel. Laid back, pretty surroundings, real pretty, and the welcoming from the ones working there matched it all.

Again, the conversation was amiable and I settled in with it, though I still couldn't get the idea of eating nettles completely out of my mind. Marilyn was as busy as a honey bee in Spring and Mel, who looked to be in his eighties, was crooked and slow-moving, but he kept coming by and regaling us with one-liners.

The other lady working there was named Patti. Clearly told me she was a single mom and both of her boys were autistic. She was also Raul's cousin. Her parents had been killed in an automobile accident when she was five years old and Raul, only seven years old at the time, had taken it upon himself to be her big brother and, in a way, her surrogate father.

Patti and most of the Nettles Gang had gone to high school together and had remained friends as the years passed, except for two years when Patti "just up and disappeared" with a stranger from Mississippi. I liked Patti. She worked hard with a smile and without a complaint, and seemed to be a good friend to everyone.

Underneath all the congeniality, however, was a low level tenseness. When anyone wasn't talking or directly listening, their eyes would furtively dart back and forth, like they were waiting.

And waiting they were. Clearly whispered to me that the man who Patti had disappeared with for two years was her ex-husband, Vernon. He was a "bad man" and in fact, was so rotten that everyone believed that Patti's kids were autistic because he beat her daily when she was pregnant. I nodded and said, "Likely the case."

Clearly then told me that Patti had gotten word that Vernon wanted to meet her at Marilyn's that afternoon, the reason being that his current wife had left him to parts unknown and for some reason, he got it in his head that Patti was behind it.

Moreover, he was just one of those "evil souls" who, every now and again, liked to beat someone senseless who offered little or no defense. In this case that would be Patti and her two boys and that's the reason Raul was there, to make sure that didn't happen.

Clearly wasn't in the least worried about Raul going one-on-one with Vernon. The worrying thing was that Mel had just told them that Vernon had connected up with a half dozen or so other guys who had similar tendencies. It was a violent gang, pure and simple, who enjoyed terrorizing the good folks of the Arkansas hill country. And right now, they were headed to Marilyn's with blood on their minds.

Clearly apologized for getting me involved but I said it wasn't necessary, that I was happy to help. (Well, maybe "happy" wasn't the right word. It was more like I was honored to fight the good fight.)

Now, I'm bigger than many and stronger than most but by nature I'm not a fighter, never have been. But there are some things I'll fight for: women, kids, the elderly, and animals. Do not like seeing them abused. I've always felt that if you're a man looking to mete out some physical punishment, find another man.

However, during my time as an MP, I did learn how to defend myself as well as how to bash in some heads when I needed to. It was a survival thing, nothing more, and as the minutes passed, those old survival skills started awakening.

So. A reckoning was coming. Seven bikers against approximately the same number of soulless gangsters. Had I been a dispassionate observer, I'd have bet on the gangsters, but because I'd connected up with the Nettles Gang, I put my faith in us.

Around fifteen minutes later, Mel told Marilyn to gather together some food and drinks then round up all the ladies and Patti's two boys and take them to one of the vacant cabins. At the same time, Raul, who was sitting in the middle of the room, nodded to the rest of us. Jerry moved to one side of the room, I went to the other. The rest wandered outside, presumably to hide until the violence began.

We waited.

———∿———

A half hour later, we heard some pickups drive up. Doors slammed. The air grew still and heavy. Followed by seven of his "friends," Vernon strode in like a starving honey badger looking for dinner. His right hand man said, "Fuck, Vern, this place is a piece of shit." The rest of them chuckled. Mel got a glare in his eyes.

Vernon stood in front of Raul's table. "Where is she?"

"Who?"

"You know who. Patti."

"Hmmm. You talking about the plump gal that was two years older than me and lived two houses down when I's a kid, or the one that was the homecoming queen the year before I graduated?"

Vernon crossed his arms. "Godammit, where is she."

"Oh, I think she up and married some big-time lawyer from Atlanta, Vernon."

"Fuck you." He seethed. "I'll find her myself. And the name's Vern, Raul, just Vern. And when we get to it, I'm gonna flatten ya like a pancake."

"That's an old metaphor, Vernon. You should come up with something new."

Vernon's nostrils flared. "Goddammit! The name's just Vern, Raul."

"Why? You get mixed up with two syllables?"

Vernon stared like he was Lucifer, red-faced with hatred and looking to destroy a city. Raul calmly took a sip of beer. "You do know what a syllable is, doncha Vernon. It's a part of …"

"Shut the fuck up!"

"… part of a word that has only one vowel sound whether it's surrounded by consonants or not."

Vernon visibly shook with rage for almost a minute. His gangster friends shuffled and furtively looked around. Finally, he took a deep breath, stretched his neck and nodded at me. "That one of yer friends?"

"Oh, I believe he owns that Road Glide with the Washington plates."

Vernon nodded at Jerry. "What about that guy? Know him?"

Raul looked over at Jerry. "Hey! What's yer name?"

Even though he was drinking a 7-Up, Jerry looked and sounded drunk. "Jerruh."

Raul looked back at Vernon. "His name's Jer…"

"I heard him, godammit!"

"Jerry." Raul took another sip of his beer. "What about the owner over there behind the bar. You ain't asked about him yet. He probably has a shotgun."

"Him? Shit, he's so old and slow he couldn't hit the side of a barn door."

Mel's nostrils flared. Raul slightly shook his head. "Another line that's as old as the hills and twice as dusty, Vernon. Maybe if you learned how to read, you could find some new ones."

Again, Vernon started shaking with rage. Finally, he said, "We'll be waiting outside." Vernon swiped the napkins and condiments off two tables as they strode out. Mel was red with fury.

I'd already formed a high opinion of Raul but after this exchange, my estimation of him grew exponentially. He intelligently insulted Vernon and actually never answered any of his questions – or more accurately answered with non-answers – which are two of the MP techniques I learned that are guaranteed to get any adversary mentally off-kilter.

Most importantly, however, he didn't react to anything Vernon said. As Mark Twain once wrote: He had the calm confidence of a Christian with four aces.

The thing is, the less you react, the more angry the other guy becomes. And the more angry a guy is, the more careless he is. And Raul had these techniques down like a veteran sniper.

Raul drummed his fingers on the table for a minute, gave Jerry a level gaze then me. We each looked back unflinchingly. He slightly nodded once then got up and stretched. We checked our knives then walked outside.

Vernon smiled maliciously then chuckled when we got close. "Shit. Three on eight and one of 'em drunk? You must be stupid, Raul."

In a flash, Raul kicked one of the gangsters in the crotch. He fell down with a plop. "Make that three against seven." Then Jerry and I immediately did the same. "Well, whaddya know. Three against five."

Vernon's bravado waned as he and his cohorts nervously backed up. After a few moments, he took out a switchblade, waited, then flew toward Raul. Raul deflected his arm aside then, like a judo master, pushed him down, making him sprawl on his face and stomach.

Jerry and I attacked the others, then within seconds the rest of the Nettles Gang joined in, hitting hard and mercilessly. It didn't take long, not even a half minute, before all of Vernon's gang was lying on the dirt either unconscious or barely able to move.

That left just Raul and Vernon, who was still sprawled, face down, on the ground. Raul kicked him once in the ribs then, with the heel of his boot, smashed the hand that held the knife, breaking at least a couple of knuckles and fingers.

He picked up Vernon then hit him in the jaw and we could hear the bone shatter. After that, Raul, taking his time, would pick up Vernon, over and over, and deliver haymakers to his torso. It was brutal and went on for minutes.

At last, Vernon was lying on his back, unconscious, Raul standing over him breathing heavily. Mel ambled over with his shotgun. "Raul, you and the rest of the guys go see how the ladies and boys are doing. I'll clean this mess up."

While walking away, we heard two shotgun blasts.

The air was comfortable as we rode back to Friendship Park, each of us contemplating what had happened. The late afternoon sun strobed through the trees, and the swooping birds and the rumble from our engines slowly brought the mood back to normal. When we got to where Earl had pulled a shotgun on us, Jerry's gas can was sitting on the side of the road, full of gas.

The festivities were waning when we arrived and all of us helped with the cleanup. Just as the sun dipped below the horizon, it was time to say good-bye to my new friends. Good, good people. The hugs from all the guys and their ladies were firm and meaningful. The bear hug from Raul is one I'll never forget.

EPILOGUE

After that day, Clearly and I stayed in touch. She liked telling me about the adventures of the Nettles Gang, a term I used but she never did, and I liked hearing about them.

It was several days after the events at Marilyn's when she texted that Vernon's seven cohorts were still nursing their broken bones and bruises. Vernon himself was still in the hospital getting ready for a life in a wheelchair. Mel's two shotgun blasts had been directed at his shins and they "pert near blew the bottoms of his legs off."

END

THE TRUTH

I know a lot of people I call friends but that's not unusual when you live in Oklahoma's countryside, what with folks always smiling and asking how you're doing. I know a lot of fellow bikers I call friends, too, but since motorcycles are a common sight in these parts, I suppose that's not unusual, either.

Now, one of them good biker people is a man about three decades younger than me. He's a friendly and helpful sort and everybody around here knows him and likes him. He's not tall, about five-five or six, and I suppose you could say that despite a somewhat small physical stature, his respect stature is big and tall. And though he teaches history and some sort of highfalutin math at the college down the road, he's a helluva motorcycle mechanic and loves to ride.

In fact, he's so good at wrenching that folks like telling a story about the time he crashed after avoiding being hit by one of them SUVs and ended up having to rewire his alternator on a rockslide during a hailstorm just so's he could get to his sister's wedding in Albuquerque on time. It's not true, of course. I'm only saying it to let you know how highly he's regarded.

His full name is Jasper Jayseel Jackson and if you think that's an unfortunate name for a biker, well, he'd be the first to agree with you. I know he would because he's informed me as such on several occasions. Of course we was drinking every time, but it don't matter because he's one of them fellas who changes naught when he's had a few or a few too many.

———∿———

About a year after Jasper's sister got married, she and her husband and their two-month-old baby girl moved out to Burbank, California. He would visit them every month or so and the little girl, Sally's her name, grew real fond of her uncle. Because he wanted to spend as much time as possible with her, he always took an economy flight instead of riding there.

One time, when Sally was about two years old, he went to visit for a whole week during Spring Break. I took him to the airport in Tulsa and remember how excited he was and how happy I was for him. He really does love that little girl.

Some hours later, he was in the Burbank Airport waiting on his luggage, just sitting there minding his own business. There was this rich fella in a real expensive suit standing next to the conveyor belt also waiting. With him was his two kids, a boy and a girl who weren't quite in double digits age-wise, and they was dressed real nice and acting well-behaved. In fact, Jasper felt they was too well behaved because they's just standing there staring straight ahead and not smiling or having any fun. Kids are supposed to have fun according to Jasper. And me, too, I might add.

Anyways, the rich fella didn't like having to wait for his luggage amidst all the people he thought were beneath him, so he started pacing around and letting out all sorts of exasperated sounds and finally went to talk with the lady in charge of the baggage claim area.

It didn't take a minute before he started yelling and saying all sorts of derogatory things about the airline and the people who flew on them, and how it was insulting to him to have to be a part of it. Well, Jasper didn't care for that at all because all he could see around him was good folks just wanting to get home.

He also noticed that as soon as the rich fella left, his two kids started acting like kids, poking fun and giggling and such, which, to Jasper, meant they was afraid of their father instead of respecting him.

After insulting the baggage claim lady every which way, the rich fella came back to his kids, saw they's laughing, and yelled at them to shut up. Well, that was another thing Jasper didn't like. There's no reason to talk to your kids like that over something like laughing. Well, whatever it was they's laughing at must have been pretty funny because the two couldn't stop. So the rich fella hit them right back of the head, first the girl then the boy.

That's when Jasper got up and walked over to him and said, "Don't hit yer kids." Now, he was all calm and not shouting or threatening or nothing, and the rich fella said, "Who the hell are you?"

Jasper looked at him and said all quiet-like, "I'm the guy who told ya not to hit yer kids." Now, you gotta admit that did answer the question but, let's face it, it ain't what the rich fella was expecting. So he looked down and up at Jasper and said, "Fucking hillbilly asshole."

Now, you might think this would've riled Jasper up but it didn't. You see, when you've been raised like most of us country folk, an unkind word or insult from someone you don't have respect for don't mean nothing, it carries no weight. So Jasper didn't react at all and just kept standing there.

The rich fella went back to pacing around and bumping into people and pushing them out of the way and acting like his shit don't stink, and when he wasn't looking, his kids started playing again. Now so's you know, the kids was playing real nice, not hurting nothing or bothering nobody. Anyways, that's when the dad made a big mistake.

He came back and yelled, "I told you to shut the hell up!" and hit them again, real hard this time. The girl started crying and the boy fell to the ground and he's crying, too. And that's when Jasper did something that got him in big trouble.

He flew at the rich fella, hit him in the face, blood's spraying out all over, and the rich fella fell backwards onto the conveyor belt just as it was starting up. He's stunned, almost passed out, and didn't notice he's riding towards that square steel opening, and when he got to it, he hit his head and started going inside. Just then, the baggage claim lady came out, pushed a button and stopped the belt from moving.

The rich fella's all twisted around and crying like a cow giving a breech birth and everybody else was laughing. They's even a bunch of people applauding Jasper and a few patting him on the back, and they all got his email address so's they could send him the videos they took with their phones.

An ambulance showed up and took the rich fella away, which Jasper thought was overkill. After all, all he had was a broken nose, a few missing teeth and a headache. The police showed up, too, and got all the information about what happened from Jasper, the baggage claim lady, and all the others who saw the whole thing.

———◆———

After it was all over, Jasper went on to stay with his sister and brother-in-law, good folks they are, and playing with Sally and helping with the housework. A couple of days later, the police showed up and arrested him for assault and battery. And that's when he called me.

The judge had set the bail at a hundred thousand – the rich fella's lawyer had wanted a half million – but there was no way Jasper could afford even ten percent of that for a bail bondsman. You see, he does make good money but, honest to Pete, gives most of it away, mostly to charities that help abandoned animals and kids in unfortunate circumstances.

He wanted to know if I'd come to Burbank and bail him out, which made sense because I do have a good-sized nest egg and I live simple. Besides, I'm retired and divorced twice and always looking for something to do and Jasper's a good man and my friend, so I flew there before the day ended. I bailed him out straightaway and got us a couple of motel rooms.

We then went to a tavern for a couple of brews and that's when he told me what happened. He even got out his laptop and showed me the videos the other people took, which is why I'm able to relate all the details.

Well, for us Okies, it was straightforward: The rich fella was in the wrong and got what he deserved. But in California things are different, what with all them rich lawyers and loophole finders and everybody having to be nice and never stepping in to stop anything bad, which there's always a non-responsible reason for. So Jasper and I figured he was in real trouble. And he was.

Jasper's sister and brother-in-law wanted him to come back to their place, but he declined because he didn't want to bring all his legal troubles to their home. Wouldn't be good for Sally, he reckoned. But he did promise to visit that little girl three times a week and take her to the park and buy her ice creams, and he did just that.

Now there's something else about Jasper you should know. Should've told you sooner but now's as good a time as any, I guess. Jasper, and I swear on my momma's grave, does not and will not allow himself any kind of lying. Not even a small fib now and again. He believes in and lives according to that old saying about how the truth will make you free and he ain't never backed away from it.

Of course, it's gotten him into trouble before because there ain't many who live by such a standard. And we got any number of California types in Oklahoma. But the way he looks at it, if he don't ever tell a lie, he'll always have a clear conscience and there ain't nothing better than that.

The next day, Jasper talked with a public defender who told him to take a deal. Otherwise, it would end up as a jury trial and there was no way he could win it because he had sixty-four cases just that week alone and the future looked much the same. And a private lawyer could end up costing upwards of a hundred thousand.

Not only that, the trial would drag on for months, maybe over a year. The public defender explained that that's one trick rich lawyers do because it makes people's lives miserable by making them miss work, which means they'll be more amenable to making a deal.

Jasper's answer to the public defender? Well, you could have expected it. "No way. The truth will save me." Now, you might think that was naive on his part, and I suppose it was, but you gotta admire his faith. The result was that Jasper decided to defend himself.

The first trial, a pre-trail or something like that, was scheduled for three weeks away. I wanted to provide moral support for Jasper so I told him I'd stay with him till the very end. Then I got an idea. I said, "Tell ya what, my friend, I'll fly back home, put our bikes on a trailer and drive them out here. Between the court appearances we'll ride around and see if California has any good roads. Get your mind off all that legal stuff."

He thought that was a fine idea and that's exactly what I did.

———✧———

The morning after I got there with our bikes, Jasper, being a history professor, said he'd like to ride up San Francisquito Canyon to where the St. Francis Dam had been, which is the site of the second largest disaster in California history and the second largest man-made disaster in U.S. history. Well, when you don't know an area, any road's as good as the next, so we took off.

We had to take a couple of freeways to get there and once we pulled onto Interstate 5, the traffic backed up. Now, we's from the country so the only thing we could figure was there must have been an accident, but that wasn't the case. Evidently, that's just normal traffic in Southern California.

There's nothing for us to do but creep along at a few miles an hour and that's when we got passed by a couple of sport bikes splitting lanes, or white-lining as some call it. After that, a couple riding two-up on an Electra Glide was doing the same and then some cruisers and more sport bikes went by.

We looked at each other, shrugged our shoulders, and followed suit. Turns out that's legal in California so we took it as at least one good thing about the state.

We finally made it to San Francisquito Canyon, immediately fell in with a group of local riders, and it wasn't long before we got to where the St. Francis Dam had been. We all pulled over and Jasper began a history lecture and I gotta say, he is one helluva raconteur.

Among other things, we learned that the dam was designed and built by a self-educated man named Mulholland between 1924 and 1926. It collapsed two years later around midnight and ended up killing four to six hundred people as the water and chunks of cement rushed fifty-four miles to the Pacific Ocean. The body of the last victim wasn't found until sixty-eight years later in 1996.

A lot of lives were saved, too, by two motorcycle cops in Santa Paula. They was just getting off work when they heard about the dam busting, so they got back on their bikes and turned on their sirens and woke everybody up in the surrounding area so's they could get to safety.

It got us all to saying that no matter the disaster or the alarming circumstance, there are always a few or a bunch of bikers who'll take responsibility and make things better.

Mulholland was found to have followed every known scientific protocol and then some, so he was never charged with nothing. The real interesting thing was that he never offered up any excuses and said that if anyone needed to be blamed, it was him and him alone. It's rare to hear a public official take responsibility like that, especially in a state like California, so we agreed he must've had some Okie in him.

We took off after the history lesson and, tell ya what, San Francisquito Canyon is one damn good cruising road. Mostly broad turns and what we found out later the bikers around there call half-twisties. Decent road surface and good views, too. And not very many cars, which was a welcome change from what we'd seen so far.

After some time, the folks we was riding with took us to a tavern called the Rock Inn in a place called Lake Hughes.

The Rock Inn is a dyed-in-the-leather biker bar. Live music, sawdust on the floor, good looking waitresses working hard and fast, a pool table, and biker-like signs on the wooden walls. It was the first time either of us felt at home since leaving Oklahoma.

We sat at a big round table with the folks we'd been riding with and after we told them where we was from, they wanted to know why we was so far from home. So Jasper, with his inability so say nothing but the truth, told them.

Well, they was so impressed with what he did to that rich fella that we ended up not having to pay for our drinks or food so I guess there are some good folks in this state.

Two of them bikers, turns out, was lawyers named Andrew Allan Allison and his wife Alison Abigail Allison ("Triple A all the way, baby!") and right on the spot, they said they'd help Jasper any way they could for free.

Then the good California folks told us about all the other great roads in Southern California but the names was coming by so fast that we could make note of only a few.

A few hours later, we said goodbye to our new friends then headed back to our motel. It was a good day for Jasper, I could see it on his face. I do like that man, I really do.

—⁂—

For the next two weeks, Jasper and I, with help from Andrew and Alison, prepared his defense at night and rode during the days he wasn't visiting Sally. Just like they said, there are some really fine roads in California providing you're willing to go find them. And we came to the conclusion that California is one helluva beautiful state and that the only thing wrong with it is that there are too many people.

Well, that and the state government which, from all the legal motions filed by the rich lawyer, seemed to favor a father hitting and verbally abusing his kids providing he's rich and can afford a rich lawyer.

The time for the pre-trial seemed to arrive in an instant. In the front of the courtroom, Jasper was sitting alone at the left table and the rich fella and his lawyer was sitting at the right. I swear, their suits cost as much as my Road Glide.

When the judge came in, we all stood, a custom with which I agree. The judge, Wendy Wells, was a blond with curly hair to her shoulders and a real pretty face, something I know Jasper also noticed, but with her robe on, you couldn't tell what the rest of her looked like, other than the fact that she was short.

I was sitting in the section reserved for observers and sitting next to me was the baggage claim lady from the airline. She's about my age and real pretty, too. Slender, nice smile, good manners. To be honest, I started liking California even more.

The first order of business was a ruling on a motion filed by the rich lawyer of getting rid of all the videos in evidence because they was inflammatory. Well, Jasper spoke right up. "Well o' course they's inflammatory! Ain't that the reason fer evidence?"

Now before I go any further, I should reiterate that Jasper is a highly intelligent and highly educated man, what with two masters degrees. But he does have an Okie accent, which I noticed had, of a sudden, become more pronounced. I reckoned he did that so's the rich fella and his lawyer would think he's stupid and not take him seriously and, hopefully, get a little careless.

It's like that old Sun Tzu Art of War thing: When you got it, pretend you don't; when you don't got it, pretend you do. The perfect example, Jasper once told me, was back in 1804 when President Jefferson and his Secretary of State, James Madison, hoodwinked Napoleon and ended up paying only forty-seven cents an acre for the 827,000 square-mile Louisiana Purchase. It was a move that absolutely saved the United States from being taken over by either England, France, or Spain, the three superpowers at the time. But, as interesting as all that is, it seems I'm getting away from the story at hand.

It turned out that Jasper didn't need to say nothing because Judge Wendy Wells refused to throw out the video evidence, and after some more specious arguments from the rich attorney, threw out the entire case. Just like that, Jasper won. But the rich lawyer, being what he is, asked for a retrial in Los Angeles County and I guess that was something Judge Wendy Wells was obliged to grant.

As we was leaving the courtroom, I tipped my hat to the airline lady and let her go in front of me. She looked right at me with the sweetest smile and said, "Well, aren't you the perfect gentleman!" That made me feel a might proud so I took leave to walk with her to her car.

Her name was Saratoga and when she found out I had my bike in town, insisted on seeing it. I told her we'd taken the pickup to the courthouse so it was back at our motel, but that I wouldn't mind meeting up with her for an ice cream sometime. She said she'd love to but that if we was gonna meet, she'd want a ride as well. Man, that suited me just fine.

We talked for a long time because Jasper had to sign a bunch of papers and when he finally emerged from one end of the courthouse, Judge Wendy Wells walked out of the other end, a fact I thought wasn't coincidental, if you know what I mean.

She wasn't wearing her robe so I could see she had a few pounds on her, most of them in the right places, but you know how most of us bikers are: we like a lot of softness to snuggle up against.

Jasper and Wendy talked for the longest time like they was old friends who hadn't seen each other in a long time, which gave me more time with Saratoga, something I was enjoying more and more.

Later, when Jasper and I was counting our blessings, I found out that Wendy took him up on his offer to ride on the back of his Heritage Softail. Not only that, they was gonna meet up on Saturday morning for Danish ice cream at a place called Paradis in a town called Montrose, which is exactly when and where Saratoga and I agreed we was gonna meet. Ain't that something.

The closer Saturday got, the more excited Jasper got. He even bought a new toothbrush, a new stick of deodorant and a new do-rag. And then cleaned off his helmet and shined his belt buckle. Of course, he wasn't the only one getting excited because I did the same.

—⁓—

We met up with the ladies Saturday morning and while we was eating some damn good ice cream, we started talking about which routes we should take. Jasper and I had already ridden some of the roads but nowheres near all of them, so the ladies decided they'd take us to one of the ones we hadn't yet been on, called Little Tujunga Canyon.

They said we could ride up to Bear Summit, then into Santa Clarita for lunch at the Saugus Cafe, which Wendy, knowing Jasper was a history professor, informed us was the oldest cafe in Southern California. This made for smiles all around and off we went.

After only ten or so freeway miles, we turned onto Little Tujunga and, dang, all I gotta say is there ain't no roads like that in Oklahoma! There was so many curves I swear I's getting dizzy, and it was so much fun that Jasper and I was hooting and hollering louder than our engines.

For a minute or so, I's worried if I could handle curves like that, but after staying upright through that fifteen foot wide hairpin that's on a fifteen percent downhill grade, I figured I could handle anything.

Of course we wasn't keeping up with Jasper and Wendy, them being younger than us, but at least we was staying within sight.

Little Tujunga kept twisting and turning and going up and down and the views kept getting better and better. I hadn't felt that much excitement in a long time and having pretty Saratoga on the back with her arms wrapped around me tight made it a whole lot better.

When we got to the second summit, we pulled over at a small parking lot next to a grassy area with a couple of picnic tables on it. Wendy and Saratoga led us up a mound and, good Lord!, looking down over the valley in front of us made me dizzy again because I's higher than any mountain in Oklahoma.

Then we headed up the five- or six-mile Bear Pass Road, rode through Los Piñetos Fire Station and continued for a half-mile or so. The road was pretty well chewed up, especially that last half-mile, so it was a slow go, but it was such a perfect day that none of us could have gotten upset even if we'd wanted to.

We got to the road's end, parked at the side, then walked on a narrow trail around a chainlink fence, across one of them army helipads and to the end of the mountaintop.

My, oh my, was that a grand sight! On top of the world it felt like. It felt so good that it was a couple of minutes before I realized I was holding Saratoga's hand. For a second, I's worried I'd overstepped my bounds, but when I looked at her, she gave me another sweet smile so I guess I's doing okay.

But we wasn't anywheres near to how far Jasper and Wendy had gone. At first they's arm in arm, then they started hugging and kissing real deep like they's in one of them romantic movies. Kept expecting to hear some beautiful music come out of somewheres.

Saratoga and I left them to their fervor and walked back to the bikes. I kept on expecting them to show up but they didn't for the longest time. As the minutes kept on passing, Saratoga kept on smiling and she finally kissed me on the cheek. I swear I's in heaven.

After that, the trip down to Santa Clarita felt like I's riding on clouds. Lunch at the Saugus Cafe was a whole lot of fun, though I can't remember nothing that happened except thinking about that kiss from Saratoga. I may be an old fella, but I remember what being smitten feels like and smitten I was.

As the days rolled by, Saratoga and I grew closer and closer, a gradual coming together of matching sensibilities on the inside but opposites on the outside, what with me being an Okie from the sticks and her having grown up on the streets of South Central Los Angeles. But passion is passion and believing is believing and they can grow inside of any two people and we was proof of it.

On the other hand, there was nothing gradual about Jasper and Wendy's coming together, something I could only witness by the fact that after that first Saturday ride, Jasper didn't make it back to the motel until Monday morning looking all worn out.

———

Jasper was arraigned the following Friday and me and Wendy put up the money for his bail, which was a quarter million this time, meaning twenty-five thousand for the bail bondsman. Officially, all the money came from me because Wendy thought it would be inappropriate for Jasper's first judge to favor him, which could put her ruling in a bad light.

As soon as we bailed Jasper out, he checked out of the motel and moved in with Wendy. When Saratoga heard of that, well, in not a week I's living with her.

As time went by, Andrew and Alison, them two lawyers we met, would come over to Wendy's a couple of nights a week and the six of us would try and figure out what to do with Jasper's lawsuit. I swear, the rich lawyer was filing so many motions that Jasper could barely keep up just signing his name. The delays kept coming, too.

With the dark cloud of his impending trial hanging over Jasper, the only things that kept him afloat emotional- and spiritual-wise was seeing his niece and riding every day he wasn't. And, of course, Wendy.

Saratoga lost her job with the airline because they figured it'd somehow stop them from getting sued by a rich fella who hits his kids. But she wasn't upset by it because she's already a retired nurse and only took the job so's to keep busy with her life.

Besides, once she started living with an Okie, she had her hands full learning the proper way to make biscuits and gravy, and getting him used to eating fried okra and black-eyed peas, with cornbread being a common food.

———

A month or so later, Wendy got a couple of weeks off so she and Saratoga decided they'd take us country boys for a tour of California. So we headed west then got onto the Pacific Coast Highway heading north. It was real nice riding next to the ocean, something Jasper and I had done only a few times before.

It wasn't far past Cambria that it began to get real pretty and when we got to Ragged Point, it felt as if we'd gone to another world made of deep blue water, crystal white clouds and flower-covered mountains. We stopped often to take photos and rest, though sometimes Jasper and Wendy would do anything but.

We spent two nights in Monterey and during the day took a cruise in the harbor and learned all about John Steinbeck, which got us to remembering all them wonderful stories of his, and we all agreed he's one of our favorite authors.

The following morning we stopped in La Selva Beach, walked a bit down a mountainside and across some railroad tracks. Jasper and Wendy found a secluded spot between mounds of grass-filled sand and Saratoga and I did the same.

Man, was it paradise being with Saratoga! I won't go into any details except to say we's two sixty-somethings making each other feel a whole lot younger by the minute. I figured Jasper and Wendy was doing the same but more of it because we got back to the bikes a whole hour before they did.

We stopped in Santa Cruz for the night and had a whole lot of fun riding that roller coaster and eating anything and everything that was deep-fried and made out of sugar. The next day we headed east to Los Banos, then the following night stayed in Buck Meadows just inside of Yosemite.

When we left the next morning, us two Okie boys got our first look at steep-angled mountains, jagged streams and V-shaped valleys the likes of which we never knew could exist. It was the kind of beauty that makes you just look and not say nothing, as if the words themselves would taint the grandeur.

The three days we rode around Yosemite was when the word love started slipping into my thoughts. And from the way Saratoga was acting, I reckoned it was the same for her. For us, it was a settling down, like the way snow does the morning after a storm, and when you look out your window, all you see is pure white stretching out forever, calling your name.

———— ∿ ————

Getting back to Burbank was like waking up from a dream, the kind of dream you was glad to have had, but feeling remorse that it's over and all you want is to have it back again. Especially for Jasper, who had a big pile of legal motions from the rich lawyer. To see a man go from the highest he's ever been to the lowest hurt me real deep.

The next night, the four of us, along with Andrew and Alison, sat around Wendy's kitchen table and gloom seemed to color everything. We'd all been motionless and not talking for a bit when Saratoga began shaking her head slightly and scrunching her lips together. Then she started tapping her foot and looking around like she's wanting to hit somebody. Then she spoke up.

Now, she wasn't needing any kind of retribution for losing her job, but she was highly indignant that a bad man who hits his kids and disrespects others could get away with sending a good man to prison. Oh, she went on and on about it, getting more and more riled up, and getting us all riled up, too. And all that riling-up led to a plan.

Jasper still had them videos on his laptop so we took a look at all of them. Most wasn't too good – could barely see or hear anything – but the last two? Everything about them was crisp and clear.

So we each emailed them to everybody we knew asking them to upload them anywheres they could think of. We did that because Wendy, Andrew, and Alison explained that if the videos became what is known as public record, then the new judge would have a real problem keeping them out of the trial.

Within days, they's everywhere seemed like. The ones on YouTube kept getting taken down but they kept popping back up, too. It had a big effect because, of a sudden, the rich fella and his lawyer was in a hurry to go to trial.

While all that was going on, Saratoga, Andrew, and Alison did some research into the rich fella's divorce. Turned out that except for visitation rights one day a month with her kids, the ex-wife got nothing, not a dime or a bed to sleep on. The rich fella's lawyer saw to that.

Now, to be completely forthcoming, the ex-wife did have an affair with an old college flame while she's married, but what got to us was that the rich fella was having affairs all along. Made Bill Clinton look like a Boy Scout.

The ex-wife's name was Linda and after the divorce, Taco Bell was the only place she could get a job. Later, she got other jobs, too, saved her money, went to night school and became a court reporter and eventually married a fella named Hans Boken, who owned a car dealership.

She and Hans seemed to be doing right fine, but being able to see her kids only one day a month had to be tough. That's when Saratoga came up with another idea.

One morning, she jumped on the back of my Road Glide and we paid a visit to Linda Boken. We showed her the videos (she's one of the few who hadn't seen them) and she was understandably distraught from seeing her kids get hit, though she did laugh a bit when she saw her ex-husband lose a few teeth and hit his head and start crying. We also told her about what he was doing to Jasper.

Saratoga left her phone number and a few days later got a call from Linda. She had talked with her husband and they was wondering if they could get the kids full time. Saratoga got them in touch with Andrew and Alison, who said they could get total custody of the kids because the rich fella's main defense was that he was a kind and loving and faithful father and husband. So they filed for a retrial on their divorce.

That was good news but what was even better news was when we found out that because the videos were circulating all over the internet, it wasn't long before the rich fella was hit with five different sexual harassment law suits and lost his job and half his money from the out-of-court settlements, which meant he had to get cheaper attorneys for his new divorce and the suit against Jasper.

The sexual harassment lawsuits caused the divorce retrial to be a real quick one, and it included full custody of the kids for Linda and Hans and alimony payments dating back to when the original divorce happened. That left the rich fella with just the one legal battle with Jasper. But that's when Jasper turned the tables. Now it was him filing the motions and the delays.

It wasn't a month later when the rich fella dropped his lawsuit. Jasper was elated and all set to leave the whole matter behind him. But the five of us wouldn't have it and insisted he sue the rich fella for lost income, court costs and defilement of his character. He finally agreed.

Again, the rich fella settled out of court, which made him as broke as a ne'er-do-well hopping trains in Oklahoma. Jasper paid back Wendy and me and paid Andrew and Alison top-dollar wages for all their help. And he still had enough left over to treat all of us to a three-week ride to the Northern California and Oregon coast.

Looking back, I guess Jasper was right all along. The truth not only saved him, it helped out a lot of other folks, too.

EPILOGUE

You might be wondering how it all ended up.

Well, the rich fella couldn't get a job anywheres, not even Taco Bell, so he went to living the life of a bum on the only thing he still owned: a boat in Marina Del Rey.

None of his friends would help him out, which just goes to prove that when you hit kids and disrespect strangers and them you're supposed to love, you ain't got no real friends.

But them videos was still having an effect and one night, someone drilled a big hole in the bottom of his boat, then it was set on fire the next night. He sold it for almost nothing and the last we heard, he was living with his parents.

Jasper and Wendy continued to live together for a couple of weeks but ended up realizing, in a good way, that they had used each other. Understandably, Jasper needed the kind of solace only a good woman can provide, someone who could take his mind off of a terrible fate that was waiting for him. Too, Wendy needed a good man to let her know she was a good woman and desirable, someone to take the loneliness out of her life.

They parted ways but are still good friends. Even though Jasper's sister, her husband and Sally now live in Tulsa, in the six years since, every three or four months, Jasper, with a gleam in his eye, will take off "to somewheres west where the mountains are." Well, I know where and why he's going and so do you.

Saratoga and me? Well, I stayed for a couple of weeks, too. Once, we rode down to where she grew up and she showed me the Watts Towers, which are real interesting, and showed me where she lived and went to school when she's a youngster. All the while, she was a little withdrawn, embarrassed maybe, and I finally called her on it.

For some reason she was afraid I'd think less of her because of her beginnings. No thought could be further from my mind, I told her, and when I took her into my arms, she folded into me, crying.

I looked around and said that it sure was a rundown area and the houses were small and there wasn't a clean spot to be seen, but that she was proof that beauty can bloom anywheres.

Then I said that her old neighborhood is a lot like the white trash area where I grew up, the only differences being that a poor black neighborhood has more people and indoor plumbing. At the time, I didn't know if it was the right thing to say, but I guess it was because she held on even tighter.

During the week after that visit, I started having second thoughts about being with her because she's such a beautiful, educated and sophisticated woman and all I am is an old piece of white trash who did a few right things in his life. So I started feeling that it wouldn't be right for me to taint her life with mine.

When it came time for me to go home, I loaded up my bike on the trailer and took off after an hour-long goodbye. An hour later I pulled over somewheres in the desert, no place special, and reminisced and ruminated for a long while. I couldn't leave. It was cutting me too deep. So I drove back and told her so and that fine woman has never left my side since.

We've been living together for six years now – never saw a reason to get married – and tell ya what, I've gotten used to eating fried okra and black-eyed peas, and Saratoga now makes the finest biscuits and gravy in Oklahoma.

END

DARLENE AND THE MOSSBERG

In 1919 in New Haven, Connecticut, Oscar Frederick Mossberg, a Swedish immigrant, and his two sons, Iver and Harold, started a new firearms company: O.F. Mossberg & Sons.

Their first product was a .22 caliber pocket pistol. Three years later they began manufacturing .22 caliber pump-action rifles. Other firearms and firearm accessories for the civilian market followed. Their profits gradually waxed and occasionally waned until August 1961 when they introduced their 500 Series pump-action shoguns, of which they sold over ten million.

The Mossberg 500s are about as simple and as light as a shotgun can be. They're solid and reliable as well and the various models are used by hunters, law enforcement and the military. The 500 HS410 "Home Security" model is the least powerful shotgun Mossberg manufactures. Nevertheless, it can cause considerable damage. Especially to a human body ten feet from the end of its barrel.

Some years ago, I stood next to my motorcycle alongside a highway in the middle of the desert and wondered, "What am I doing? I mean,

I don't even know where the hell I'm going. I get this 'no destination' thing. I do. Embrace it even. But you'd think I'd at least go somewhere, anywhere, where it isn't so hot. Arizona smack dab in the middle of summer on a motorcycle? What was I thinking?"

When I had started out in Southern California two days before that, everything was fine, really fine. Exhilarating almost. Beautiful day, temperature in the mid-70s, light breeze every now and again. Perfect.

But summertime in Arizona? I swear, the air was as hot and heavy as a steel furnace in the Sahara Desert.

I'd been divorced for six years, no girlfriend, and the twins were all grown and on their own and doing well, which meant that I was on my own, too. So I figured I'd ride around the country for a couple of weeks, maybe three or even four. Something I'd always wanted to do.

I was between jobs so no problem there. Had the money, too, which was pure luck. Got a winning scratcher for three thousand dollars and when I turned it in at the 7-11, I bought another scratcher and it was good for another five thousand.

But that Arizona heat was killing me. Felt like I'd been tarred and feathered without the tar and feathers. It was too early to get a room so I decided to stop and cool off at the next diner, which ended up being only five miles down the road, just north of Flagstaff. It was also too early to start drinking so I just got some fries and a cold lemonade.

Darlene was the waitress and, man, was she friendly and cute. Sloe-eyed, long and wavy black hair, ready smile. Easy conversation, too. Five-four or -five and maybe twenty pounds overweight, but she still had a small-ish waist and a not-too-big butt. Many would considered her way too top-heavy but it was a helluva combination as far as I was concerned. Pure "meat 'n' potatoes" like my Uncle Matt used to say.

The place was only moderately busy but Darlene was the only one serving the patrons and, dang, was she having to move fast. Despite her busy-ness, however, she kept stopping by for short conversations when she wasn't filling up water glasses or taking orders or serving food and drinks.

I enjoyed her company so much that the fifteen minutes it usually takes me to eat a plate of fries and drink two glasses of lemonade turned into thirty minutes. Then an hour. Then an hour and a half and another plate of fries and more lemonade.

Like I mentioned, Darlene was friendly, wonderfully so, but there was something else. It showed up in her eyes, the way she would occasionally gaze into a far beyond. I sensed it as a sort of sadness or maybe a distant anxiety in the back of her thoughts. I'd no idea what caused it, of course, but the more we talked and the more I watched her, the more I became aware of it.

That sadness or anxiety, or whatever it was, combined with her undiluted sweetness fetched my imagination, and a desire to really get to know her began bubbling up.

We never had a conversation that lasted more than a minute or two. But the thing is, in life, when your opportunities are short and few, you make the most of them, right? And that's what Darlene and I did. By five o'clock, it was like we were old friends, joking around and poking fun and such.

At one point, she leaned on the counter in front of me, showing off a cleavage that reminded me of the Grand Canyon. "Where ya staying at?"

"Haven't found a place yet."

She looked down the bar to her left then back at me, the smells of frying food from the kitchen filling the air. "I'm taking a month off of work." She looked down and fiddled with her silver keepsake bracelets. "I live a couple of miles down the road. Small place but I like it. It's nice."

Now, even though I've known my share of ladies, I was never good at picking one up. Never really knew what to say, how to break the ice, so to speak. But that's when I was on the prowl. Here, Darlene was making the move which, let's face it, is an unusual situation for most any guy. My thoughts were redlining and the only thing I could think to say was, "Love to see it sometime."

Darlene half closed her eyes, smiled a sultry smile, then straightened up and pushed out her breasts farther than she had all day. She then gave me one of those straight-to-the-loins come-hither looks. Man, oh man! And what a fine vision it was, watching her sashay back to her customers.

———

When we got to Darlene's, she parked her Toyota to the side of the garage to make room for my bike. It didn't take long for the hot-and-heavy to start. In fact, as soon as the garage door closed, she stepped over and started getting friendly. Really friendly, if you know what I mean. The stroking, the low and guttural moans, the languishing eyes. Soft kisses on the neck. It all quickly escalated into a fervid to-and-fro. When we finally walked into her house, we were each covered with nothing but sweat.

Darlene grabbed a couple of cold beers and we sat across from one another on the couch. That distant sorrow, or worry or anxiety or whatever, showed up again along with that faraway gaze. I watched her as silent minutes passed.

Then in an instant, she was "back," and like women often do, she began talking, telling me her story, the good and unfortunate things from her past.

It was during her first marriage that she found out she couldn't have any children. Her husband was a good man but he definitely wanted kids, three or four at least, and wasn't at all interested in adopting, so they divorced.

Her second husband never passed up a chance to berate her for her infertility and a number of other things, too. Even hit her a bunch. The last time – they'd been married for two years – he put her in the hospital for some days, which caused him to be arrested.

When she got home, there was a note from him on her dresser that said he was going to kill her some day. She divorced him, something for which I praised her, and it finalized on the same day he was sentenced to prison.

There was a third husband, too, and though he was a through-and-through loser, he also looked down on her because of her inability to be a mother. That marriage didn't even last six months.

Though she'd always wanted a husband, a permanent one who was a good man, she had come to the conclusion that marriage wasn't in the life's hand she had been dealt. Because of that, since the end of her third marriage, she had taken on one or two lovers a year, always shying away from getting an actual boyfriend because it may lead to another marriage.

While listening to her sweet voice, I came to realize that, despite all the misfortunes in her life, Darlene's most dominant characteristic was how utterly good-natured she was. Not an unkind word passed her lips, even when she talked about the abuse from her second husband. More and more, however, I wondered what it was that took her "away" to that melancholy place.

We had just started our third bottles of beer when she walked back out to the garage. I followed. She went over to my bike and began stroking it like she had done to me earlier, walking around and around it, admiring and feeling every part.

She got a towel out of the dryer, folded it, then climbed on top of the gas tank, rested her back on the towel on the handlebars then gave me another come-hither look. I climbed onto the seat and the moment I entered her, she said, "Start it up."

For the longest time we sat still, coupled together, becoming more and more aware of the slight shaking of the engine snaking through us.

———⁓———

I've always felt that the best sex begins with the fourth time, occasionally the third, but definitely by the fourth. By then, any self-consciousness is gone, we both know what the other looks like, all the flaws and the plus-points, and we know the things that turn the other on. And so it was with Darlene and me early the next morning. Despite the layers of dried sweat and bad breath, we went at it like porn stars on amphetamines.

After showering and getting dressed, we went for a ride south on Highway 89A. Man, having Darlene on the back was like being guided by a real-life guardian angel. The way she leaned in perfect parallel with me, held me with the right amount of snugness, how she'd point out wildlife and nooks of beauty. And those huge breasts constantly pressing into my back just amplified the pleasure.

Highway 89A has only one lane either way (my preference) and what a satisfying route it is. Sheltered and cozy with friendly trees, the rumble of my pipes, and a canopy of soft blue sky.

Just before Sedona, the number of cars quadrupled. At least. We'd originally thought about having lunch there, but the number of tourists and the packed-in traffic disabused us of the idea, so we kept going to Jerome.

When we got to Jerome's small commercial area, we parked alongside the road, then walked down the embankment a bit where we sat arm in arm for the longest time, admiring the view.

As the minutes passed, I began to see that view as a reflection of Darlene herself. It wasn't so much the eye-catching aspect of it, rather how the hills were soft, caressing almost, and the air crystal clear. Peaceful.

We talked about the many things we still wanted to do with our lives. As the conversation lingered, I was again mesmerized by her wholesomeness, her undiluted charm, her ability to see everything with a sort of serenity.

I took another long look at the view in front of us. The way the hills in the distance rolled up into a hazy blue were like her plans, her desires. They were there and known, just not yet well defined.

We enjoyed a long lunch at a small cafe right there in Jerome and continued talking about this and that. She asked about my marriage and kids and old girlfriends. She told me about her old boyfriends and lovers. Trouble we got into in high school. Brushes with the law.

We took off mid-afternoon heading southwest to Prescott, and after the road leveled out a bit, we pulled over to stretch the legs. She grabbed a blanket out of my right saddlebag, took my hand, then led me to a copse of low trees on the other side of a low hill. After she laid down the blanket, we lost our clothes and, just like that, we were getting all friendly again.

Afterward, we were lying angled to each other, buck naked and silent for the longest time, the air still and comfortably warm. She said, "You know all that stuff I told you? About my second husband and getting hit and all that other bad stuff?"

"Yes."

"Well, don't go thinking I'm feeling sorry for myself 'cause I'm not. The way I look at it is we're each given a life and it's up to us to make the best of it."

"And that's what you're doing."

"Yeah. I have friends, good ones I can trust, and a job I like and make good money at. I mean, I'm not totally living in paradise or anything but I'm getting better at it all the time."

"Sure you'll never get married again?"

She gave me a lighthearted smile. "You hinting?"

I laughed lightly. "No. I'm a lot older than you. You don't want that."

"Maybe so." She checked me out from top to bottom. "But you look damn good for an old guy."

Boy, could that woman make me smile! "Well, I'm not that old. I'll be forty-seven next month. But you've got to be, what, mid-twenties?"

"Twenty seven."

"Twenty years difference is a lot." I got a mischievous look. "Of course, if I were a really rich guy with a big yacht I could talk you into it."

96

She crawled over to me then laid on my chest, her breasts spreading out like whipped cream. She kissed me. "Dream on, Casanova."

We laid there holding each other for a long time, not saying anything, every now and again the silence broken by chirping birds. When the sun touched the horizon, she looked at me all dreamy-eyed and said, "I've always wanted to make love while watching the sun set."

———

It was full-on nighttime when we got a cheap room in Prescott. We didn't get dressed after showering and stayed naked for the rest of the night, except when I put on my jeans when the pizza delivery gal showed up. It was an easy evening, no strain or trying to impress.

We were lying on the carpet – it was close to midnight – slowly catching our breath after the sixth or seventh time of going at it. Darlene stared at the ceiling with her now familiar faraway look. It was like she was looking at gray memories or watching scenes from some black and white movie.

"He's getting out in three days."

"Who?"

"Frank. My second husband."

"He's still in prison?"

"Yeah."

"Think he'll come to see you?"

Her voice was monotone. "Oh, he will. Won't be pretty either. He's been sending me threats for a year."

"Threats?"

"Yeah. His cousin goes to see him once a week and Frank tells him what to tell me. He has him send texts from one of those throwaway phones so they can't be traced. I already checked with the police."

"Like what? What kind of threats?"

"Beat me up. Cut me up. Rape me. Whatever."

I sat up with a start, my eyebrows scrunched. "Why not change your number?"

"He'd just come by and leave notes. Don't want him around."

"Can't you leave? Go somewhere where he can't find you."

"He'd find me somehow. Not running. Gotta face it someday. Better sooner than later."

My mind was racing. For one thing, I couldn't leave her alone. It wasn't that I was in love or anything, I wasn't, but I did care and care a lot about her. Besides, I had to be back home in three and a half weeks. What then? What if Frank waited until after I left? I mean, I couldn't guard her forever.

Her voice cut into my thoughts. "That's why you have to leave the day after tomorrow. Don't want you around. He'll kill you."

"Darlene …"

"He likes knives. He liked saying a lot that cutting somebody is more satisfying than shooting them."

"Sweet guy. But I can't leave you alone."

"You can and you will."

"But …"

"No. It's my battle. Mine alone."

Arguing wasn't going to get us anywhere so I offered a compromise. "Okay, how about this: I stay with you for a week. If he doesn't show up, he probably won't and you'll be okay."

She gazed into my eyes like she was looking through the scope on a sniper rifle, as if she was saying, "Oh, he'll show up. A week, a month, a year, doesn't matter. He'll show up." She closed her eyes then slowly opened them. Her face had softened and she half-smiled. "Okay. One week on one condition."

"What?"

She crawled over then whispered into my ear. "You keep fucking my brains out."

———~———

The next morning, we backtracked to her place in Flagstaff. It wasn't far, fewer than a hundred miles, which meant we had time to kill, so we decided to brave the crowds and have lunch in crowded Sedona. When we got there, however, we opted for only ice cream cones.

We agreed to leave my bike in her garage for the entire week. That way, if Frank did come to visit, he wouldn't know I was there so if he had any violence planned, and he most likely would, I could at least surprise him.

I hadn't packed my Ruger because, well, when I had taken off I didn't know where I was headed and without a license in some states I could get busted. I regretted the decision but so it was.

We continued making love but not with the same fervor as before, what with always being worried about Frank catching us in the act. Let's face it, if that had happened, we'd have been dead-to-rights. Not that we would have been doing anything wrong, we weren't, but the idea of me, a forty-seven year old, buck naked man going up against a young-ish hardened criminal just out of prison who likes cutting people didn't sound like it'd end well for me. Or Darlene.

When we weren't sleeping or making love, we continued talking nonstop, mostly about each other, and I learned even more about that sweet woman. Her favorite dog when she was growing up was a mutt named Max. Purple is her favorite color. She tried out for the cheerleading squad at the end of her junior year in high school but didn't make it.

Her parents – "They were always real good to me" – passed away when she was twenty-two. No brothers or sisters. She makes a killer lasagna. She'd already visited twenty-seven states and wants to visit the fiftieth on her fiftieth birthday.

A lot of other things, too. Her favorite movie (Casablanca), her favorite book (Silas Marner), her favorite historical figure (Voltaire), and her favorite artist (Cézanne).

While all of this may sound boring, it was anything but boring for me. There was a fascination, a sort of emotional thrill, to getting so non-sexually intimate with someone, something many never do unfortunately. Plus, that playful innocence of hers that pervaded everything she said or did was as if she rested on the wings of angels, ineffably light, pulling me into her world.

Add to all that the impending and possibly violent confrontation with her second husband made me want to be some sort of outlaw saint for her.

Darlene wore her distant look all day on the last day of that week. Understandable. I tried talking her into letting me stay for another week but she wouldn't have it. Wouldn't even consider it. There was nothing to do but leave the next morning, which made me feel like a bastard. And a coward.

On the way out of town, I stopped at the diner where we met. The coffee and the atmosphere were as bland as my emotions, so I left after only fifteen minutes.

Even though I was on an interstate, it was slow-going because I pulled off at almost every offramp to sit and wonder if I was doing the right thing. I ended up in Seligman for the night.

All evening, my thoughts were a gray dullness, and I could barely taste the pizza and lemonade I'd had delivered. I went to sleep early.

———~———

Around midnight, I woke up with a start. Something was wrong and I knew it. I jumped out of bed, packed and loaded up in a fury then rode back to Flagstaff like a jet stream. I got to Darlene's less than an hour later but parked a block away so if Frank was there, he wouldn't be alerted by the sound of my pipes.

I ran down the alley behind her house then climbed over her fence. The back door was locked but I could hear Frank's threatening evil voice and what I assumed to be Frank's cousin's ominous laughter. Darlene's cry was muffled, like she was gagged.

I didn't know exactly what to do but I did know that my only chance to come out of this alive, or even just partially intact, was to surprise them, so I grabbed a big rock from the backyard garden and hurled it through the back window. I heard Frank say, "Check it out." I ran around to the front and hid in a neighbor's yard behind a big cluster of rosemary bushes.

Frank's cousin spent maybe five minutes looking around and finally went back inside. After I'd crept back to the back yard, I heard him say, "I swear, Frank! There ain't nuthin' nowheres!"

I crawled through the broken window then hid behind the wall separating the kitchen and the living room. I couldn't see either Darlene or Frank, but I figured she was sitting on the couch and Frank was standing in front of her.

His voice was venomous. "Trying to fuck with me? Trying to fuck with me, bitch?" He slapped her over and over and over, then it sounded like he punched her in the stomach. She gasped.

He then slapped her some more. "Before we're done, darlin', I'm gonna cut your nippies off and watch you suck the milk out of them big titties." He and his cousin laughed. I heard him punch her three more times. She haltingly cried as she struggled to breathe.

I peeked around the side of the wall. The cousin stood at the other end of the living room not ten feet away from me, his laugh an evil snicker. I closed my eyes, took three deep breaths then bull rushed him, smashing his head on the front doorknob. He went unconscious.

Frank came at me like a madman, a crude prison knife in his right hand. I rolled into his legs, and as he fell, he sliced a cut into my back. We both got up and he came at me again.

I, too, went forward but dropped down and again rolled into his legs. He fell down again but then reached over and cut a deep gash in my left hamstring as I pushed him away with my right foot.

I instinctively crawled toward the kitchen. Frank struggled to get up but at the same time, his cousin came out of his stupor and struggled to stand as well. Their legs tangled, Frank fell toward me, and his cousin fell back against the front door.

The boom of the first cartridge out of Darlene's "Home Security" Mossberg was like a pound of TNT exploding. The following pump action was like a distant echo but the sound of the second shot about knocked me out. It seemed like minutes before I could lift my head and look.

The cousin leaned against the front door. The crater in his abdomen was big enough to cut him in two, and his blood fanned out like a flow of lava.

Frank was on his back, limp like a rag doll and with about the same amount of life. His upper chest was nothing but a chaos of red and black. Both of his eyes were gone along with much of his face.

I laid my head back down for what seemed an eternity. A warm puddle of blood slowly grew under my back and left leg. As my hearing came back, I found not a small amount of satisfaction in hearing Frank moan and mumble in abject pain.

Soon, I could hear Darlene quietly crying. I rolled onto my stomach, then crawled to her with my arms and one good leg. I lifted myself up and rested my elbows on the couch next to her.

After I undid the gag in her mouth, she took big halting breaths for a full minute. She covered her face with her hands, tears flowed through her fingers. She wore only panties, one side of which had been cut apart. There were about two dozen cuts on her breasts and her sides, including circular cuts around her areolae and a deep one on the side of her right breast.

She took her hands from her eyes, sniffled, then looked at me. "How'd you know?"

I shook my head. "I don't know. Just did." We were silent for a long time. "Where'd you get the shotgun?"

"Hid it behind the cushions. He came at me so fast I couldn't get it out in time." She started crying again. "He cut all my clothes off and started cutting me. Said evil stuff over and over." She continued sobbing. "God it hurt! I wanted to die."

It was a long time before one of us – can't remember who – called 9-1-1. The EMTs arrived within minutes and the cousin was pronounced dead just after they got there.

Frank was still alive, barely, and was the first one taken by an ambulance. He'll be in prison for a long time and most likely will never see again. But if he's "lucky," a quack student of plastic surgery will someday try to give him some semblance of a face.

Darlene and I rode in the same ambulance to the hospital where we stayed in the same room for the rest of the night and the next. While we were there, a cleaning crew went to her house and made it spotless. The police were professional and efficient and the matter was cleared before we left the hospital.

I stayed with Darlene for the two weeks before I had to get back to work. The cut on my left hamstring healed nicely though it took a week for the stiffness to mostly go away.

Darlene's knife wounds healed in little time but the dark bruise covering her entire abdomen took a while. She was sore and stiff for days and days and days.

We made love just once more, the night before I left. Understandably, we moved slowly and carefully. We both knew our affair was over but there were no second thoughts. No words, either.

EPILOGUE

The next and last time I saw Darlene was six years later. I was again in Flagstaff – in the fall when it's cooler – where I went to a sporting goods store to buy some bungee cords. She was waiting in the cashier line and when our eyes met, I smiled as big a smile as I could.

She smiled demurely then looked at the floor. She pulled out a piece of paper and a pen from her purse and hastily wrote a note, which she gave to the cashier.

When she looked back at me, she was still smiling but shook her head slightly. It was then that I saw she was with a man, about her age, and a boy who was about five and a girl who was, I'd say, close to ten. I nodded.

They left before I did and when I went to pay for the cords, the cashier gave me her note. It said:

7-11, 1/2 mile north.
One hour.

102

When I walked into that 7-11 one hour later, Darlene was already there. She put down a 12-pack of Dos Equis and two bags of chips on the floor, then gave me the longest and most gentle hug.

When we let go, her face radiated contentment. I said, "You look good, Darlene. Happy."

"I am."

"That was your husband?"

"Yes."

"Good man?"

"The best."

I nodded. "The kids?"

"Abel and Maria."

"Adopted?"

"Yeah. But I'm their mom."

I took a deep and satisfying breath. "They couldn't have it better."

END

LECTURES

Now I'm no polished raconteur and I know this ain't a good way to start a story, but I first gotta tell ya about where we live, the "we" being myself and my good friend, Flynn Kinslow. You could say that, being a biker, it's foremost on my mind and I need to get it out of the way so's I can get to the story I'm about to tell.

We live in the hills of Western Washington not far from the Pacific Ocean, and if there's such a place as God's Country, well, it'd be right here. It's so pretty around here that after the missus passed on, one of the few blessings in my life was to transplant myself from Georgia so's to be close to the kids and kidlets. And it's the same reason Flynn ended up being my neighbor, him being originally from Michigan.

Though neither of us grew up in this area, I can say that over the last six years, we've ridden every fine road the Northwest has to offer. I mean, they's all over the place and every one of them is as pretty as could be. Curvy, too, and in decent shape and surrounded by so much growth that when you sit on your bike, you just know it cain't get no more beautiful.

Flynn and I became in-sync riding partners right off, being that we each like to rest as often as the other, don't drink but every now and again, love our kids and kidlets, and ride at a good pace but not crazy. Well, except for once in a while taking some curves like we's in our twenties and on sport bikes.

Now, Flynn is a writer. Or an author. One of the two, cain't remember which. Maybe both. He once explained the difference but it eludes me right now, so I'll just say that he has a way with words, all of which he wrote himself, that made him famous with bikers and cowboys and countryfolk and, well, I guess everybody except sophisticated, college-educated big city folks. Anyway, his pseudonym is Jackson Armstrong and, well, you already know who he is so there ain't no need to introduce him any further.

His fame didn't really explode till some years back when he won that writing award that was named after a husband and wife whose last name was, I believe, MacArthur. Something like that. And that's when all the big city, college-educated folks learned his name and college professors started talking about him and analyzing him and writing about him.

But I swear, from everything they wrote, you'd wonder who they was talking about. I mean, they's making up stuff about what he really meant but didn't actually write. You'd think they would have at least read a paragraph or two of his.

After getting that award, he did a bunch of radio and magazine and newspaper interviews. Even went on TV. But as far as I could tell, all those celebrity goings-on didn't change Flynn none, which is one reason I admire the man.

Well, this introduction has gotten longer than I wanted it to be, but there's just one more thing I gotta get out of the way and that is to introduce myself. The name's Jefferson James but everybody calls me Jelly.

———⌒∾———

This story's from about two years ago. The air was cool-crisp and the sun had set. Flynn and I were sitting on my back porch drinking hot cider when he asked if I'd be interested in a three-week ride. Man that sounded good so I agreed straightaway.

It turned out that Flynn had been asked to give a couple of writing seminars at a big university in Michigan. He'd stopped giving seminars some years before that because , because according to him, most every college kid is only interested in making easy money and not learning how to write, which made it mostly a waste of his time. But the professor asking him was the son of a good friend from way back, so he said he would.

Besides, Flynn claims that going to school to learn how to be a writer is as big a waste of time and money as there is, that any would-be writer would learn more about writing by becoming a plumber, a dockworker, or a short order fry cook. You know, live life, get to know the ups and downs of it.

Anyways, Flynn figured that that seminar was a good enough reason to ride to Michigan. Not that Flynn or I ever needed a reason to ride but if one presented itself, heck, we'd take advantage of it.

So on one Spring morning – damn, the air was spanking new! – I rode over to his place and we took off. Once we got over the mountains, we headed east and by the time we crossed the St. Joe River, we was riding with a dozen others and there wasn't one face without a smile.

We all stopped at a place called Cruiser's in Stateline for lunch and it was just what we was looking for. As with most biker places, everyone was a friend, stranger or not. In fact, the place is so friendly that even dogs are welcome.

Afterward, we headed north and into Idaho's panhandle and, man, is it pretty there! We rode that scenic byway that hugs the shore of the Coeur d'Alene Lake like ice cream on hot cherry cobbler – twists and turns and friendly folks all along – and spent the night in Sandpoint. All along, the air was so invigorating that we could not get enough of it, and the green-covered hills just made us want to keep riding forever.

We got up with the sun the next day and decided to do nothing but get in some miles. Though the highway was just two lanes, the traffic was such that we never had to slow down, and we made only one stop before getting to Missoula, where we had a light breakfast.

Afterwards, we jumped on an interstate and, tell ya what, what a straight-up rush that was. I mean, we kept riding and riding and doing nothing but, and only took breaks for gas and trail mix. We ended up covering about eight hundred miles, getting into Medora, North Dakota around midnight.

We's pretty stiff the next day – actually, we's real stiff – so we took a leisurely ride through the Badlands to see some bison and loosen up a bit. It did loosen us up some but afterwards we's still so tired that we's unable to make it to the Minnesota border. It weren't no worry, though, because we still had more than enough time before that seminar.

The farmlands we rode through was real pretty and all the folks we talked with was a might friendly. Some of them recognized Flynn as Jackson Armstrong and he always took the time to talk to them but mostly he'd listen to their stories. Ain't no secret why he's so popular.

Some days later, we spent the night in Houghton in Michigan's Upper Peninsula, then rode up to Copper Harbor the next day. Now, I gotta say that that Highway 41 is one of the prettiest riding roads I've ever been on. The way it curves its way through the trees is like a gift from Mother Nature.

When we rode back along the coast of Lake Superior, there was families picking wild blueberries right alongside the road. What an inspiring sight that was. It got me to thinking that God's Country must be sprinkled all over, not just in Washington.

———

A few days later, we ended up at a nice motel about ten miles away from the university, settled in for a nap, then had a good steak dinner. Afterwards, we talked and drank a bit, bourbon and beer for me, Beefeater and tonic and a few beers for Flynn. We said goodnight around midnight and went to our respective rooms.

Flynn wanted to get to the university early so's to say thank you to the professor for the invitation, Winston his name was, and to make sure his computer was properly set up to a big screen.

Plus we figured to run into traffic so we took off over an hour before the start of the seminar, which was at one o'clock. Well, there was no traffic at all and we got there with an hour to spare. We parked our bikes and walked onto the campus thinking to get something cool to drink before heading over to the literature building.

We was walking along the grass toward a walk-up counter and as we got closer, I saw a sign that said we's entering something called a Safe Space, and another one about Trigger Words. Didn't know what any of that meant but I ain't college educated so I didn't worry about it none. Flynn didn't say anything about them but I knew he saw them, too, because he's a lot more observant than me.

We walked right through that Safe Space and to the walk-up counter. Well, being bikers we's used to people being friendly, but when we smiled and nodded to the students, they just turned away. Couldn't figure out why.

I got a root beer, Flynn got a lemonade and we sat down and enjoyed them. But it was a strange half hour because even though we was smiling and trying to be friendly, everybody kept ignoring us and walking away. Eventually we's the only two left.

Now, a safe place sounds nice. We all like being safe, right? But after Flynn explained what it meant and seeing what was going on around us, I began thinking otherwise because they's places where you have to act and talk all nice according to whatever somebody else thinks is okay.

And if you wanna talk about something that might make somebody uncomfortable, you hafta warn them first, which is what that "Trigger Words" thing is all about. And it got us to agreeing that our idea of safety is best, it being packing a handgun.

———

Flynn's lecture was to be in two parts, the first one being that day, Tuesday, and the next one the following Thursday. When we got to the room where the seminar was gonna be, we met Winston, who seemed to be in his early thirties. He was all full of enthusiasm and real nice and welcoming.

Flynn set up his computer in only a minute or two and once the seminar started, ooo-wee, was he in his element! He's pointing out stuff about writing that I could never have imagined. At first, like he said it'd be, only a few of the thirty or so students was interested. But as he went on, more and more got caught up in Flynn's enthusiasm, the original few looking like they's being handed the keys to paradise.

When the lecture was over and all the glad-handing and love-your-writing was done, we walked back to our bikes and found out we'd been issued two citations. One was because our motorcycles was too loud, and the other was for intruding that Safe Space.

There was also a security guard there, big fella, who said he's to accompany us to meet some sort of university official. Well, neither of us was interested in that but he had such a pleading look on his face and in his voice that we ended up saying okay.

On the way there, Flynn started talking with him and with his way of getting to be friends with anyone – that is, anyone he wants to – before we's half way there, the three of us was smiling and joking.

Turns out the guard, Craig was his name, and his lady had been bikers when they was younger but, like lots of folks, had to give it up when the kids started coming along. But they promised themselves that when their four children had grown up and moved out, they'd get a "big ol' Harley and ride around the country."

That's when I told him Flynn's pen name. He stopped and stared for some moments then said, "Sheeit." We's real good friends after that and it turned out that Flynn, or should I say Jackson Armstrong, was Craig's favorite author and he promised to sign all of Craig's books when we came back on Thursday.

When we got to the administration building, we went up an elevator to the fourth floor, then Craig knocked on a door with a sign that said Student Communications. After a half minute, we heard a voice say, "Come in," so we did.

There's eight students there, six of them young and two good-looking older ladies, and a middle-aged fella sitting behind a desk, wearing a sweater and glasses and fiddling with papers. Without looking at us he said, "Sit down."

Well, Flynn kept standing, which told me he's in no mood to be agreeable or conversational, so I kept standing, too, which made the university fella uncomfortable.

Finally, the university fella scrunched his eyebrows and said, "So Mr. Kinslow and Mr. James…." Now I'll just stop right here because this told me and Flynn that that university fella didn't know that Flynn was actually a famous award-winning writer and/or author.

Anyways, he continued, "We maintain the highest standards of respectability at our university and one of our rules, an ordinance, is that loud motorbikes are not allowed on the premises. And that includes the parking lot."

We didn't offer up any excuses and just said, "Mm-Hmm," which made the fella flustered.

After some moments, he said. "So uh, your motorbikes were loud enough to upset some of the students."

"Mm-Hmm."

"And also, the way you're dressed represents things a civilized society doesn't condone."

"Mm-Hmm."

"Like drunkenness and the objectification of women."

"Mm-Hmm."

"And violence."

Flynn pulled back his vest and took out his Sidewinder. "You mean like carrying something like this?"

Well, the university fella about jumped out of his seat and the students started backing up into one another. Meanwhile, Craig and me were doing our best to not start laughing.

The university fella's eyes and mouth were wide open and it was like he couldn't move. Finally, he said, "I insist you disarm yourself right now!"

Well, as you'd expect, the university fella's demand didn't mean nothing to Flynn because he just said, "Mm-Hmm," and put the gun back in its holster. Besides, exactly where was Flynn supposed to disarm himself? Out the window? The trash can? Run down to a bathroom and throw it in a toilet?

The university fella was still wide-eyed. "Well?"

Flynn just stared at him all calm-like and sighed. That's when I thought I'd make a joke to lighten up the mood, so I pulled out my Ruger and said, "Don't y'all worry none, I'll keep him in line!"

I swear, it was all that Craig and Flynn could do to not double up from laughing. But then I felt a little bad because some of the students started crying and the university fella was trembling.

After the university fella regained some composure, he slammed a folder full of reports in front of us. We reached over and began reading them and, I gotta tell ya, it was hard to believe they was written by college students because most of them was scrawled like they was written by a drunk on death row.

And some of the sentences was so bad you couldn't figure out what they said. Bad spelling, too. Like this one. "why r criminels alowed on r campess???"

We finished reading all the reports, put them back into the folder and didn't say nothing. After a bit, the university fella violently shook his head and said, "Just leave and don't ever come back!" And that's what we did. Except we still had that second seminar on Thursday, but neither of us mentioned it.

After we rolled our bikes out of the parking lot, we soon noticed we's being followed by a white Prius with two people in it. We never did get a good look at them but it wasn't bothering us none. It wasn't long till we found what looked like a nice, food-serving tavern, walked in and got a couple of beers.

Some minutes later, the two older ladies who'd been in that group of students showed up. (It'd been them in that Prius.) I wasn't expecting them to talk to us. Heck, I figured they'd leave once they saw us. But they came over and introduced themselves as Chamomile and Savannah. We offered to let them sit with us and, to our surprise, they accepted.

Flynn put his attention on Chamomile, which was fine by me because I's liking what I saw in Savannah and from what I could tell, my interest was reciprocated.

Flynn asked Chamomile if her parents actually named her that when she's born. She smiled and said they did but it was one of her middle names. Flynn looked at her with a half smile. She was a little demure and finally said, "My first name's Rosamunde."

"Like the ballet based on Schubert."

"Yes," she said with a look on her face like it was the first time she'd ever been charmed.

"And King Henry II's favorite mistress."

The volume of communication she sent with a silent raise of her eyebrows and a slight tilt of her head!

When I introduced myself to Savannah, she giggled sweet-like and asked why I's known as Jelly. I said, "Well, get me laughing good and take a look at my belly and you'll know." She, too, angled her head a bit then said, "I just might do that."

We all ordered salads. Flynn and me got beers while the ladies had just water with lemon wedges. When our food came, they got serious of a sudden. They told us that they didn't approve of guns on their campus, didn't approve of guns at all, and that the way we was dressed was upsetting to some.

We said okay, we understood about the guns, but there's nothing we could do about the way we's dressed because we's on the road and what we's wearing is about as good as it gets.

We kept up with the friendly talk but no matter how much Flynn and I tried, we could never get the ladies laughing or even smiling. Instead, they kept talking about how bad guns are and how bikers are outlaws, but when we tried to get them to tell us what makes an outlaw an outlaw, it wouldn't go nowheres.

So Flynn offered up the definition that an outlaw is someone who lives by his own rules and those rules are ethically higher and more disciplined and more magnanimous than the laws of the land. Well, the two ladies didn't even acknowledge that.

So the conversation kept descending and getting more serious and tedious and we's both figuring it'd be the last time we'd ever see them. Then, out of the blue, Chamomile said that none of it mattered because it's all in the past – again we didn't mention the lecture Flynn was to give on Thursday – and right then, the whole air just seemed

112

to lighten up. And, not surprisingly, that's when they started asking about motorcycles.

It turned out that neither of the girls had ever been on one and the more we talked about it, the more they wanted to find out what it's like. So we decided that the next day, we'd all go for a ride.

So's to not make a long story any longer, I'll just relate that we met up with the ladies for dinner, and Flynn spent the night with Chamomile and I did the same with Savannah. And it was a fine time for all of us.

The following morning, the temperature was on the cool side but the four of us was bundled up good and, all in all, it was a fine day for getting out. First, we headed north then west on a highway next to the Grand River.

There was cars all along but we's never bothered by any of them, and the views wasn't bad at all, what with a lot of healthy farms and small settlements with mom and pop stores and steepled churches made out of red brick.

We had a light and late breakfast next to the Flat River in Lowell, then later some Irish stew at a place in Muskegon. Afterwards, we went to the Harley place in the area and bought the ladies some t-shirts, which they thought was delightful. Flynn and me was having a real good time but to Chamomile and Savannah, it was an adventure of a lifetime.

We'd originally wanted to make it to the shores of Lake Michigan, but the day was getting on so we turned around and headed back so's to avoid commuter traffic in Grand Rapids. Besides, the ladies was getting tired.

For the second night in a row, neither Flynn nor I had to sleep alone, but Chamomile and Savannah left early the next morning to get to class on time. After they's gone, Flynn and I had breakfast and talked for a bit.

Neither of us was willing to go to the university on anything but our bikes, though we decided to leave our guns in the saddlebags. And there was nothing we could do about the way we's dressed.

The more we talked about it, the more we became certain that the only right thing to do was to act like we would normally act, show up early, and walk through that Safe Space and get something cool to drink, it being a free country and all. So that's what we did.

What happened was much the same as the first time and we ended up sitting alone. It got me thinking that because none of the students was willing to say anything direct, they must be cowards and I said as such to Flynn and he agreed. And then I said that if they's cowards, then maybe having a Safe Space made sense in a way. He agreed to that, too.

When we got to the lecture hall, I figured word must've gotten around at how good Flynn is at public speaking because there's about four times as many students as before. Every chair was filled and there's even a bunch standing up in the back and along the sides. And all the English professors was sitting in the front row. After Winston introduced Flynn, he took over and, man, was it a beautiful thing to see.

He went right into what he called the nuts and bolts of writing and how all great art depends on the proper manipulation of the basics. He constructed and reconstructed sentences on the big screen and showed how even the slightest change can greatly improve the telling of a story.

And then he went into a whole discussion about the proper use of prepositions and conjunctions and how they can clarify things and keep the narrative in its proper sequence. And the switching around of paragraphs, and the erasing of unneeded sentences and phrases and why you'd do that, and the advantages and disadvantages of writing in present and past tense. (I wish I'd taken notes because this story would be a whole lot better.)

After he's done, he answered everyone's questions then thanked Winston and the rest of the faculty, too, and even the students for being willing to listen to him "flap my gums." And he signed autographs and shook paws and listened to everyone's compliments. Tell ya what, I's never so proud to have a friend.

When we's on our way to the bikes, Craig, the security guard, saw us and came running over with a smile that was so big you'd think his face was gonna break open. He had all of Flynn's books and Flynn signed all of them right there.

But then Craig got this worried look and told us he had to give us each two more citations for parking our bikes in the parking lot and for being dressed the way we were while walking through that Safe Space. And we's to have another sit-down with another university official.

We told him not to worry because we had no quarrel with him. So we followed him to the administration building but this time we ended up on the top floor. It was a bigger room and there's a lot more students there, including the guy we talked to on Tuesday, and our two lady friends who weren't looking pleased at all.

The lady running the meeting, Ms Hampton, was sitting behind a big desk just staring at us all unfriendly-like. She asked us to sit and we did because she's a lady so it was the right thing to do.

Then she started lecturing us on the evils of guns and bikers and how we's representing all the bad things about the country and we had no place among people who represented all the good things. Flynn and I just kept saying "Mm-hmm," over and over.

It was when she told us that there was this MacArthur winning writer who gave the second part of a seminar that day, and he might have seen us and gotten a bad impression of the university, that I started smiling.

But Flynn didn't react at all and I figured he's waiting for the right time to set everything straight and when the time came, man, did he say what's what.

It happened after she'd said everything she wanted to say and asked if we had anything to say in response. Flynn looked at her for some moments, then took out his wallet and handed her his business card, which has both his real name and his pseudonym on it. From the look on her face, you'd think a hog giving birth just dropped on her desk.

Flynn let her grab a bit of composure then said, "You're right. We did come back to your campus for a second time riding our loud motorcycles. It is also true that we walked through the Safe Space again and had cold drinks. The reason we did those things has to do with respect, of which your 'Safe Space' students have none. And by that I mean respect for others as well as self-respect.

"The character weaknesses your policies engender are a disservice to the university, yes, but mostly to the students themselves. Their inability and/or unwillingness to engage either me or my good friend in a simple conversation is proof of the cowards you have created.

"I say that because people are not born with such cowardice, rather it is taught, and that is, indeed, something you have done well."

The afternoon sun sliced through a window warming up the room. Flynn took a deep breath. "About the guns. It is true we always travel with them but whenever we have been asked, and asked politely, to not bring them into a public establishment, we have always complied and will always do so. But that courtesy was not extended here."

"About the way we dress. We're on the road and, as my friend often points out, what you see is about as good as it gets.

"But from where or from whom, may I rhetorically ask, did you get the idea that dressing like this is a sign of lawlessness? Or disrespect for others? Or any of the other things of which we have been accused? If you know the definition of bigotry, then you know how utterly bigoted those assumptions are."

Ms Hampton sat frozen with her mouth open. Flynn quietly sighed then said, "It is because of all this, that I and my friend do not acknowledge your ordinances, nor do we intend to act in accordance with any penalty you attempt to inflict.

"Last, if I had been asked to wear a suit, I would have had to decline the invitation because I don't own one. And if you didn't want us carrying our guns, all you had to do was ask. Unlike you, we do have respect, for others and ourselves."

We waited a few moments but Ms Hampton sat motionless with a blank stare. Well, no reply was forthcoming so we got up and left. Craig walked with us and when we got to our bikes, we shook hands with the good man and wished each other well.

Then, right as we's leaving the parking lot, that white Prius started following us again. We rode for a few blocks or so till we came to one of those gas stations with a big parking area. We pulled in and Chamomile and Savannah pulled in right after us.

The four of us stood there not saying nothing for a few minutes. Finally Chamomile spoke up. "Those were harsh words you said back there." We just looked at her all calm and peaceful-like. She went on. "You hurt some feelings, too, and I don't think it was very nice."

Now, in a way, she did make two good points because Flynn had been harsh and did injure some feelings. But looking at only those two things is ignoring the broad picture. Flynn said, "True, the words were harsh and I can see that feelings were hurt."

"So couldn't you have said what you wanted in a different way?"

"I could have, yes."

She glared at a loud truck as it rumbled by. She looked back at Flynn and said, "But you didn't."

"That's correct."

"Why?"

"Because of what I said earlier, Chamomile: Respect. Ms Hampton, the other fellow we had a meeting with, and the students all judged

116

Jelly and me only by the way we dress and our preferred transportation. Furthermore, they all assumed an elevated status while doing so. That, as I said, by definition, is bigotry.

"And why did I say my peace in a direct, and perhaps harsh, manner? Because I don't respect people like that. They don't deserve politeness." His eyes and smile took on an amused and understated air. "As you may expect, I don't mollycoddle."

He looked at Savannah then back at Chamomile. "Now, you and Savannah here are a bit different. You disagree with us about guns, true, and that's fine. But you did not voice your opinions as ad hominem attacks, and that's why we're willing to talk and be with you.

"In contradistinction, the reports from the students and the quasi-lectures by the university's officials were directed at me and my friend in a personal way, so for them, I offer no tolerance."

Chamomile and Savannah looked at each other for some moments like they's thinking it all over, for the first time taking in the big picture, I's hoping.

Me and Savannah walked away and had ourselves a conversation. She said she'd never before looked it from our perspective and had never thought about how rude we'd been treated. And she apologized, which made everything fine by me. And when I looked over at Flynn and Chamomile, it seemed like they's coming to the same understanding.

———※———

We all had a nice dinner and an enjoyable night after it, and Flynn and me left the following morning taking the superslabs southwest to the Rockies. We didn't stop for any sightseeing 'til we got to Ouray. We rode the Million Dollar Highway and, looking around, I figured I's right when I had that thought about God's Country being all over.

We spent the night in Silverton and after we finished having a quiet breakfast the following morning, I looked over at Flynn and said, "Seems you got something on your mind."

He said, "It seems like you're thinking the same thing I am."

"Well, I brought it up first so it's your turn."

Flynn smiled that friendly smile of his and said, "I'm thinking I'd like to get on home and see the kids and kidlets."

"I'm with you on that, my friend. Let's get to hauling."

END

GEORGE AND FRANCIE

No one likes George. Really. Whenever his name comes up, sure, people will say things like, "Oh you'll get used to him," or "He's not really that way," or "Somewhere under there is a heart of gold." The truth of the matter, however, is that none of those are true.

Basically, George is a functioning alcoholic, which isn't that unusual, but the thing is, even before he began drinking all the time, he was pretty much an ass. And that's why his only real friends are Jim, Jose, and Jack, the last names of whom are Beam, Cuervo and Daniels, or as he likes to call them, my BCDs.

George has been a bartender for the past thirty years and one of the many reasons no one likes him is that he can't (or won't, which is more likely the case) mix any drink properly. Except Mai Tais. Those he does well, really well. But anything else? He's so bad he'll screw up a straight shot of Fireball. But everyone else has learned to keep their mouth shut because they don't want to be the target of his terrible temper, which is the only reason he still has a job.

Deals is the name of the restaurant/bar he works at and over the years it has become more and more an odd place. In the beginning, it was a steakhouse, a nice one, too, with ranch-type furnishings.

Some years later, without changing the menu, the owners tried a Polynesian decor (huh?), then a 40s Casablanca theme and most recently, a sort of open-air, upscale industrial look. But they never quite got there because through all those years, they kept the old and cracked red leather booths and the even older carpet.

Nevertheless, the steaks are tasty, as is the house dressing, and they recently added a short vegan menu, which didn't change the number of customers or the income, but it did make the owners feel more with the times. You have to wonder, though, why a steakhouse would offer vegan entrees.

Getting back to George. Though he continually screws up nearly every order, the other three bartenders keep most of the patrons happy and despite its shortcomings, the place does a healthy business. Old regulars and newer customers enjoy their meals and most of them properly tip the old and young servers, who never quite fall in with the required dress code. Especially bosomy Francie.

Francie is one of the older servers. She makes excellent tips and is also a three-times-a-week manager. When she arrives on Mondays, Wednesdays and Thursdays, she'll immediately take off her old, worn-out green jacket and, braless, walk around in flip flops, tight jeans and a loose-fitting tank top. And every time George first sees her, he scowls, "Well, I guess Sloppy Tits decided to show up."

———✺———

The four bikers sitting at the Deals' bar are Mark, Jay, Freddie and Bam. They're vets from Desert Storm and wear the patch proudly on the backs of their vests. They're part of a larger veteran's motorcycle club but ride with the others only on special occasions, the reason being that they are way more than just weekenders. True to their natures, during the nine to ten months of riding season, they'll do upwards of fifteen thousand miles.

It's during the summer months when they put in most of those miles. They'll take off for weeks and weeks at a time to New England, the South, Alaska, the Midwest, Mexico, wherever they decide, and they do it all on routes based on nothing but what-the-heck-why-not. One interesting tidbit is that of all the hundreds, maybe thousands, of bars they've gone to, they have gotten into only one fight.

It happened at a large and busy place outside of Baltimore. It wasn't a biker bar per se but, let's face it, any bar is at least partly a biker bar, right? Anyway, there was a group of seven college football players, big guys, who were laughing hysterically while one of them said derogatory things about a rather large lady whose husband had just passed out from drinking.

As you may surmise, the bikers didn't like that, so Mark nodded at his three friends. They spread out. Mark then walked up to the abusive student and politely told him to quit with the insults and apologize. He and his friends laughed. He said, "Shit, that fat, ugly bitch should be thankful we even noticed her." Well, if you know Mark you'd know that that was the wrong thing to say.

Mark flew at him and broke his jaw with the first punch. Before the other six football players could react, Jay, Freddie, Bam and the rest of the bikers in the place descended on them with an ungodly wrath and a minute later, all seven jocks were lying on the floor in various stages of shock, pain, and injury.

After the ambulances took them away and the police got statements from everyone, the four bikers helped the waitresses clean up the blood, broken glass, and busted tables and chairs. They then gave the owner eight hundred dollars for the damage. It was the right thing to do and they all agreed it was money well spent.

Despite that one time, they make friends wherever they go, which is understandable being that bikers are generally friendly. In fact, these days, whenever they ride away from Southern California, hardly a day goes by when they're not riding with at least a few new and old friends.

They live a tad north of Los Angeles and during the non-summer months will go to Deals after their day rides and have a beer or two or three while listening to George complain, his most favorite target being Sloppy Tits.

This particular Thursday is special because Mark had gotten word that his son, Peter, an Army Ranger at the end of his fifth tour in Afghanistan, just stepped onto a flight that will bring him home and home for good. The four men clank their beer bottles together often and congratulate Mark on raising a fine son.

Peter arrives home the following Thursday and the following Saturday morning, as a coming-home present, the four men give him his very own, perfectly operating, black and chrome Harley-Davidson FXRT. The young man is overcome with emotions, thanks them all profusely, and when he finally settles down, the five of them go for a ride into the mountains.

It's an early morning on an ideal autumn day, what with the mountains of Angeles Forest cutting into the dustless blue sky and the rumble of five Harleys ripping apart the air. The curves seem to fly by as they ride in perfect formation, Mark leading then Jay, Freddie, Bam, and Peter.

At the third stop, Jay and Freddie tell Peter he ought to lead for a stretch, as a sort of homage to his new bike. But he declines saying, "Nah. You guys're the experts, I'm still learning."

This sits well with the men and Mark gets approval looks from the other three. But no matter how hard they ride, Peter keeps up with them, something else that makes his father proud.

The fact is that Peter is a fine young man, through and through. Old school manners, competent, impossible to fool, and a hard worker but teenager-type fun to be around.

After a visit up to Mt. Wilson, they make it to the northern end of Angeles Forest Highway, head west on Sierra Highway, south over twisty Little Tujunga Canyon, then east on the 210 Freeway. They roar into the Deals parking lot as the sun sets.

After they remove their helmets, Mark has a word with his son. "The bartender, George, is an ass and won't like you, but don't pay him any mind."

"Okay. Does he like anybody?"

"No. And no one likes him, either."

"If no one likes him, why do you keep coming here?"

"Well son, it's true that we don't actually like George, but there is something we do like about him."

"What's that?"

"He doesn't give a damn what anybody thinks."

The five men sit in George's section of the bar. He brings over four beers, then looks at Peter for some seconds. "Who the hell're you?"

"Uh, name's Peter."

George grunts, walks away, comes back with a bottle and whips it along the bar to Peter. It bangs against his arm and spills onto the bar and his pants. George glares at Peter a moment then walks away.

Francie, her sloppy tits slopping all over, sees this and comes running over with a towel and a smile. "Oh you poor boy, let me clean that up for you." She vigorously wipes the bar and the front of Peter's pants, apologizing all the while. When she's done, she says, "There you go, Sweetie!" and kisses him on the cheek.

Peter watches her walk away then says, "Damn! That woman needs a bra. A big one, too." The four men laugh and Bam, originally from Alabama, says, "And a long one, like one of them air socks at the airport."

George brings over a second round and duplicates his serving of Peter, except this time, Peter catches the bottle. The third round is much the same and after that, the five men head on home.

They ride in the mountains several times every week and every time they stop to stretch their legs, Peter looks at the spectacular surroundings and at his bike and his father and his friends, and realizes more and more the freedoms he fought for.

As the days pass, George never does show Peter any kind of civility, but it's not a bother because he never shows any kind of civility to the others, either. In fact, the interactions with him always become a humorous end to a day of fine riding. Life is good.

Francie, however, is another story. She really takes to Peter and with the two decades difference in the their ages, you'd think it'd be a motherly type of interest. But it isn't.

She truly feels it wasn't that many years ago when she was "Francesca Dawn, Exotic Dancer" (i.e. pole dancer and stripper), and was bringing home up to a thousand dollars a night. She also feels that the years have been kind to her and with enough makeup, she'd be a fine addition to any man's life. All in all, however, her endearments are more annoying to Peter than George's growling and disrespect.

Thanks to Jay and Freddie, Peter gets a good paying job maintaining the trucks at the local delivery firm where they work. With a good and regular income and a military loan, in just three months, Peter is able to buy a nice two bedroom house on Chantry Flat Road in the hills north of the city.

———∿———

Along around this time, some local yokels watch a TV show about outlaw motorcycle clubs. They're impressed at how tough those one-percenters are so they decide right then and there to start their own club.

The thing is, despite watching that show, they don't know much about one-percenter bikers. Almost nothing, actually. But they do know that they need a name that won't piss off any of the ones already in existence. After days of "brainstorming" and arguing, they finally decide on Hog Sack Packers.

The biggest problem the eight of them have, however, is that only five of them own working motorcycles. Two small Yamahas, two small Hondas and a tiny 125cc Kawasaki Eliminator. Two of the others have old Harleys that are missing parts and gathering rust so they ride around together in an old pickup. The eighth one rides an old and rusted, black-smoke chugging ATV.

Now, while all this is rather comical, please understand that they do have a mean streak that sometimes borders on dangerous. They have shotguns and handguns and one of them, after hearing about "something called samurai," bought a handful of shurikens at a garage sale. And they sell drugs, mostly meth and pills, to local high schoolers, which is how they earn a living.

Once they decided on their MC name, their favorite pastime on the weekends became causing the trouble they thought one-percenters should, one afternoon shooting at neighborhood pets. (They didn't hit any but did scare a few folks.)

They also get into fights at local bars, all eight at once, and verbally abuse women, especially those with boyfriends and husbands. And they do their fair share of scoring the sides of cars, smashing windows and starting small fires.

When the patches they ordered online arrived, they had a celebration, none of them having a clue that they had misspelled their name on the order form as Hog Sak Pakers. They even got President, Vice President and Member patches. They didn't have vests and didn't know how to sew, and didn't know anyone who could, so they duct taped them to their flannels.

Some while later, they found out that one thing one-percenter motorcycle clubs do is claim a territory as their own. They had a meeting about it and after three six-packs decided it would be best to gradually approach that particular aspect.

After five more six-packs and a good amount of pot, they decided that a certain eight miles of Chantry Flat Road was theirs, one mile for each member, and nobody could ride a motorcycle on it without their permission. And those eight miles included Peter's home.

The following Monday morning, Peter is on his way to work when he comes upon a roadblock of sorts. He stops and turns off his engine. It's a pretty funny sight, what with an old pickup, a rusted ATV and five small bikes. The President is standing in the bed of the pickup and announces in an official tone of voice, "You are hereby warranted by the Hog Sack Packers that you are no longer unallowed to be not transferring this here road."

This doesn't make any sense, of course, and Peter cocks his head to the left and looks at him with a furrowed brow. "Huh?"

"You heard me. We let you go this time but next time there'll be hell to pay."

The five with motorcycles roll their bikes out of the way, two of them bumping into one another. Peter shrugs his shoulders, starts his bike, then takes off. By lunchtime, he had forgotten about the incident and for the rest of the week rides Chantry Flat to and from work without incident.

However, after midnight the following Sunday, the eight wannabe one-percenters break into his house, beat him up, make a mess of his place, breaking all the furniture and his brand new TV, and yell into his ears to never again mess with the Hog Sack Packers. They also spray paint Hog Sak Pakers on the living room wall along with what is supposed to be a hog with a devil's head.

After they leave, Peter shakes out the cobwebs, takes an assessment of the situation, figures it's something to deal with the next day, and goes back to sleep.

Peter's late to work and when Jay and Freddie see his black eye and bruises, they immediately want to know what happened. He tells them, the word immediately gets back to Bam and his dad, and they all decide to meet at Deals after work.

It's just before sunset when the five of them are sitting at the bar. George looks at Peter and asks, "What the hell happened to you?" Peter tells him and he asks, "Whatcha gonna do 'bout it?"

"They're not getting away with it, that's for sure." With that, George hands him his beer.

Then Francie, crying like a girl who just lost her puppy, comes running over. She hugs and kisses Peter and tells him it'll be okay, over and over, and the more she does so, the more embarrassing it becomes.

After he finally gets her off him and onto a stool, Peter tells them everything that happened the night before. He also tells them about the roadblock the Hog Sack Packers had set up, which brings some smiles and chuckles to the men and Francie.

The first order of business is to find out who the Hog Sack Packers are and where they live, which they figure has to be close to Peter's house. Francie says she's off during daylight hours and volunteers to hang out at his place to see if the wannabe one-percenters come by again.

George says, "No way. Ya don't know who these guys are and with you there all alone, you'll be a sitting duck to fuck."

125

"Well, what do you want me to do, then."

"I'll stay with ya."

Francie plants her hands on her hips. "You?"

"I'll bring a coupla shotguns."

Mark speaks up. "That might work. Peter's place is too much of a mess so he's staying with me and the wife until we get this settled."

On Monday morning, George shows up at Peter's with two shotguns and Francie brings a small TV. They watch daytime shows and take turns napping but none of the Hog Sack Packers ride by. It's the same every day for the rest of the week.

After Deals closes that Friday night, they sit with the five bikers and tell them about the absence of the Hog Sack Packers. George says, "Well, there's only one way to find 'em and that's to ride a bike up and down that street 'til they come out of their hole."

Francie replies, "And who's gonna do that? Peter's staying with his dad and they all have to work every day."

"Well, if I still had one of my old bikes, I'd do it. Love to meet up with them peckerwoods with my twelve-gauge."

"Oh shit, George. You don't know one thing about riding a motorcycle."

"The hell I don't."

"Yeah, right. I've known a lot of bikers over the years and know one when I see one. I even have an old Shovelhead in my garage." She smiles coquettishly. One of my regulars gave it to me years ago after a special weekend I gave him just before he went to prison. He got beat up later and died so I just kept it. Anyway, there's no way you know how to ride."

"Shit, woman. I was a flat track racer when I was in my twenties and won a bunch of trophies. They's still at the house gathering another layer of dust every year."

Francie's eyes grew large. "Really? Did you know Calvin Smarts or Hale Jensen? They were two of my regulars."

"Cal and Hale? Shit, we went at it a bunch fer years and never stopped beating each other a bunch. Hated 'em and loved 'em. Where's you working back then?"

"Calypso's in Eagle Rock. Where'd you hang out?"

126

"The White Stallion in West Covina. You know a lady named Brandy? We lived together a while. Dorothy and Charlotte, too, if ya knew 'em."

"Never knew a Dorothy or a Charlotte. I knew Brandy but we were never friends."

George frowns. "How could ya not be friends with Brandy? She's one of the sweetest pieces of ... sweetest ladies I ever knew."

"She was a bitch."

"And I guess you were Miss Goldilocks, huh?"

"I treated my men right."

"Bet you did, too, for the right price."

"Damn straight. A girl's gotta get her own any way she can."

George shook his head. "Still can't believe you never got along with Brandy. And she's sweet to everybody, not just customers."

"She had a better ass but my tits were bigger, so there was no way we'd ever like each other."

"She did have a nice ass. Perfect it was. And if you were to ever pack that rack of yers in a bra and show some cleavage, you might still git some looks."

Francie steps back, hands on hips "Oh, and you don't look over at me every time I take my jacket off. Every time I bend over, too. If I'm so undesirable, why do you do that?"

"Oh hell, that's just old habits."

"Well 'old habits' this, you old fart." And right then she takes off her tank top like a pro. The five bikers cover their eyes and collectively say, "Oh gawd," but the cleaning crew stops and ogles. George, too, spends some moments taking in the view.

The next day, George goes over to Francie's place and, sure enough, there's an old Shovelhead in the corner of her garage. He spends four days checking out every nut, bolt, screw and seal, puts on new tires, and comes to admire the workmanship of whoever originally fixed it up. The paint job, too.

By Thursday morning, it's all back together again. He washes it down, kicks it once and it starts right up. He puts on his riding gear and rolls it onto the driveway, excited about the first riding he's done in twenty years.

But Francie is standing in his way. Hair drawn back under a purple and black helmet, sunglasses, black high-heeled boots, tight-ass jeans, and a packed rack that's bulging out of a twenty-year-old leather jacket. George stops and stares. She looks such that he gets an itch in a place he dare not scratch.

He asks, "What t'hell you doing?"

"It's my bike. I'm going with you."

George ponders the scenario, thinking he never thought Sloppy Tits could look so good. He takes another down and up look at her, then comes to the conclusion that it's actually not a bad idea. So he has her jump on the back and off they go.

Man, are they having fun. For two hours, they ride around the area and on the freeways while George gets back his old skills and works in the tires. Finally, they head up Chantry Flat.

Now, if you know Chantry Flat, you know it deadends at the top and the only way back down is the way you came. A section of it is pretty damn twisty, too, and once they get into it, George keeps hollering, "Yeah, 'at's it!" and Francie screams the three times he drifts through a curve.

They get to the top then lie resting on the ground. They talk and laugh about the old days when they hadn't a care in the world except for having fun and responsibly being irresponsible. A couple of agreeable hours later, they head back down Chantry Flat for a late lunch.

When they're next to Peter's house, they come upon a Hog Sack Packers roadblock. George says, "Shit. Shoulda brought the twelve gauge." He turns off the engine.

The Hog Sack Packers president is standing in the back of the pickup. In an imperious voice says, "Y'all ain't warranted fer transpiring this here road and from here on out, ya'll ain't not unallowed as per the decree of the Hog Sack Packers."

Like Peter, George and Francie furrow their brows and wonder what that means. But whatever it means, George says, "Fuck you."

The vice president, a big guy with missing teeth looks at Francie's deep cleavage and says, "'Course, if ya wanna hand over yer lady friend, we might come to an agreement."

"Fuck you."

"Well, okay then," the President says. "But you been warned."

"Fuck you."

The small bikes part, George kick starts the engine and he and Francie ride through. When they get around a corner, they pull over and watch the wannabe one-percenters head up Chantry Flat then turn left on a dirt road a half mile later.

———— ～ ————

That night at Deals, George and Francie recount the event to the five bikers. Mark and Peter are ready to crush some heads, the others, too, and they all agree that Saturday night will be the time of reckoning.

Mark says, "Now we already know what has to get done but there's one thing we need to do first and that's find out the lay of the land, so to speak, and make sure we know exactly where those miscreants will be."

It's a sound idea, so before sunrise on Saturday morning, Jay, Freddie and Bam dress up like they're going quail hunting and jump into Bam's pickup. They drive down the Hog Sack Packers' dirt road for a hundred yards, pass an old rusted tractor then thirty yards later, come to a dilapidated old house.

Next to the house is an open-air, brick-lined fire pit, the front of which is littered with empty beer cans. Bam continues driving then parks behind a low hill about a half mile later. They pretend to be hunting, shooting their rifles into the air now and again, but keep their binoculars on the house.

It isn't long before a couple of men come out and look to where the shots are coming from. Figuring it's the Hog Sack Packers, the three friends wait until the sun clears the mountains, drive back, and when they get to the house, four men holding shotguns stop them.

The president says, "Y'all's on private property."

Bam, in his best Alabama accent, speaks up. "Aw shit, we dint know. Hear that guys? We messed up." He turns back to the president. "We's real sorry. Never hit nuthing so's nuthing's lost, nuthing's gained. Won't happen again, fer sure."

"Yeah, well jes make sure it don't. Ya don't wanna rile up the Hog Sack Packers."

"Oh hell no! We's leaving right now!"

Saturday night rolls around and after Deals closes, the six men and Francie, with the bikes loaded up and strapped down, ride up Chantry Flat, turn onto the dirt road, and immediately cut off their engines and park.

Mark goes over the details of the plan. "It's just going to be a good beating and then we're going to get the money to fix Peter's place back up. That's it. No guns unless it gets out of hand.

"George, you and Francie stand watch on the road and make sure none of them escape. And stay out of sight. We'll be coming at them from three sides so if one of them runs, he'll be heading straight for you.

"Jay and Freddie, you're on the right; Bam and Peter, you're at the rear. After you're all in place, I'll walk right up to them from the left and start a conversation. When you hear me say 'hell', come in and come in hard, screaming like berserkers."

Fifteen minutes later, everyone is in place. The Hog Sack Packers are all outside drinking beer, sitting around a small bonfire. Mark walks up and in a friendly voice says, "Well dang, I just went out for a walk and didn't think anybody was around here. How are you fellas?"

The president says, "Who the hell're you."

"Oh, I just live up the road a bit and was looking for some fresh air."

"Well, get the fuck out. We're busy."

"Well, okay. But you think you could spare a beer or two? This dirt road got me a little thirsty."

"What'd I just say? Get the fuck out!"

"Oh hell now, there's no…"

And with that, five men converge on eight. Mark goes at the biggest guy, puts him on the ground with one punch and commences beating his face, blood spurting out of his mouth and ears.

Peter goes straight for the president, busts his nose, punches out several teeth and kicks him in the ribs. Bam corrals another one who was reaching for a shotgun, breaks his wrist with his boot and kicks him over and over in the gut.

Jay and Freddie each take on two, but it's relatively easy as all of them are crying, asking for it to end. But it doesn't.

The vice president is running down the road when he runs into George's roundhouse right that knocks out the rest of his teeth. This puts him flat on his back. George sits on his chest beating him left-right-left, while Francie kicks him over and over in the groin.

All in all, it lasts but a couple of minutes. George grabs the vice president by the ankles and drags him back to the others. When the eight of them have been set in a line, Peter gets a hose and washes them down. Most are groaning and a few are crying.

Mark speaks up. "Okay, now you guys hurt one of us and messed up his house. We've paid you back for the beating but now you need to pay for the damage." He looks at Peter. "How much you figure it is?"

"'Bout three thousand."

"Hear that? We're going to need three thousand bucks and we're going to need it now."

The president starts crying. "Aw shit, man, all's we got is thirty-eight hundred."

Mark pauses a few moments wondering how stupid a person can be. "Well, we messed you guys up pretty good so I guess we'll settle for the thirty-eight hundred."

The president thanks Mark for his charity and so do the others, except for the vice president, who can only moan and hold onto his crotch. The president gets the cash then holds it out for Mark, who nods his head toward Peter. "It belongs to him."

Peter takes the bills, counts them and it totals forty-two hundred dollars. Out of principle, he smashes the president one more time in the jaw.

Peter tells them, "Take off all your flannels and throw them on the fire." Now all of them are crying loudly. When all of the flannels and patches have turned to ashes, Mark says, "Don't you ever, ever, ever even think of yourselves as bikers again. If we ever see any of you on two wheels, you'll find out what real hell is like." With that, the men turn and leave.

They're half way down the road when Bam stops and says, "Where're George and Francie?"

The others stop and look around. Mark says, "Wait. Hear that?"

They listen. Jay and Freddie nod and Jay says, "Sounds like a dog whimpering."

Freddie says, "It's coming from over there, behind the tractor."

They all tiptoe to the other side of it.

Francie is on all fours and George is on his knees behind her, and they're working it like a couple of nineteen-year-olds. The men stand and watch for a minute, holding in their laughter, then turn around and walk to their bikes.

Right before starting up their bikes, Bam says, "Y'know, when I's a kid I worked on cattle ranches in Kansas and Nebraska every summer for six years, and of all the hundreds of thousands of cows I seen, millions even, I ain't never seen one hanging that low."

END

ASSASSIN AND THIEF
(THE BALLAD OF WILLMONT ABSAROKA SMITH)

"Where the hell is Brad?" Charlie is pacing. Arms crossed, face in a scowl. He's normally an easy-going guy, but he does like things well-ordered and predictable. "He hasn't even answered his phone."

Nuno looks around the parking lot. "Hell if I know."

Now, it's true that no one likes to wait and Nuno is no exception, but he does have more patience with such things and seldom gets annoyed with others' foibles, having grown up among a large extended family where nothing ever started on time and disagreements had a way of working themselves out. Besides, he's still nursing the last of his caffè mocha.

"Probably banged his new girlfriend all night and woke up late." That's Max. He's loyal, sometimes to his detriment, and Brad's oldest friend. While he still respects their friendship, he has long since moved on with his life and softened his defenses of him.

"Doesn't matter," Charlie says. "He's the one who wanted to meet up early and we all of us made it on time and here we are wasting good riding time outside of a damn Starbucks."

Max, Charlie, Nuno, and Brad ride together every weekend. Well, every weekend when the weather is good, like it is today. They always meet up at the same Starbucks then ride thirty to forty miles to a local watering hole. Today, however, Brad had wanted to get an early start and ride to Neptune's Net on the coast just north of Malibu.

"I say we take off without him." Charlie is still irate.

"Nah, let's give it another five minutes." Nuno is still nursing that coffee.

"Yeah, five minutes sounds good." Max has a few bites left on a croissant.

"Five minutes, that's it." Charlie, still pacing, face still in a scowl, arms still crossed like a foaming-at-the-mouth Marine drill sergeant.

Brad shows up twenty minutes later riding his lime green Street Glide that's painted with flames, jokers, and naked women with huge breasts. Ape hangers, LED lights along the frame, Classic Rock blaring out of 150-watt speakers. He's proud of the bike because, in his own mind at least, it's the way real bikers paint and decorate their bikes. He's disheveled and smiling.

"Where the hell have you been?" Charlie asks.

"Oh, just had to take care of a little personal something, know what I mean?" Brad's smiling as he walks into Starbucks.

Charlie can't hold himself back. "Well, you could have at least taken a shower."

The three friends go back to waiting. Charlie paces, Nuno is lost in his thoughts, and Max is taking in the scene around them.

Soon, a rider on a black and chrome Road Glide rides in. Charlie and Nuno notice him but don't pay him much mind. Max, however, watches him closely. The efficient way he dismounts and takes off his helmet and gloves, and the way he walks, as if he isn't looking at anything but is aware of everything.

Some minutes later, Brad comes out with a tall caramel espresso and a blueberry muffin. "You're all as quiet as church mouses. 'Bout as ugly, too."

"Shut up," Charlie says.

"That would be mice, not mouses," Nuno chimes in.

Max sighs and says, "Brad, did you see that guy walk in a few minutes after you?"

"Yeah, that tall chick with the big tits noticed him, too."

"Ever seen him before?"

"Nope."

"Wonder who he is."

"Just some guy who wants to be like us."

Max sighs again and says to himself, "I do not think so."

One thing you should know about Max is that he comes from a long line of observers of people, something his ancestors called Witnesses. It's a tradition he takes seriously and holds in high regard

He's good at it, too, and even though he's in only his thirties, he's gotten to the point where he can tell a person's age within a year or two and which state they're from. And while his three friends continue their banter, he can't stop thinking about that tall stranger. Something about him.

Some minutes later, the stranger walks out and over to his bike and casually looks around, sipping a small coffee. Tall, slender, sandy hair, erect back, gray and quiet eyes. Max watches him and one of the first things he realizes is that the man is aware that Max is doing just that.

Max knows that observing people doesn't necessarily mean doing it covertly. In fact, one of the first things he learned from his father was that witnessing is best done out in the open. Furthermore, according to his own sensibilities, he feels that watching someone on the sly is a rude thing to do. So he walks over.

"Nice day, isn't it?"

"It is that."

"Riding alone?"

"Seems so."

Max briefly looks at the few clouds above."Where you headed?"

"Hadn't thought about it. New to the area."

Max figures the stranger was a military brat and had spent most of his youth in the south. "You from South Carolina?"

The stranger's eyebrows flick up. "Spent most of my childhood there. But we was all over."

"Army?"

"Yeah."

Both men look around for a short while, each aware that a sort of kinship is forming. A quick, cold breeze sends a chill up each of them. Max notices Brad throwing away his coffee and half the muffin. "We're getting ready to take off in a couple of minutes. We were going to head out to the coast but we got a late start so we'll probably end up at the Rock Inn in Lake Hughes. You're welcome to join us."

The stranger looks at Max, his face softening a little. "Be pleased to."

Max goes back to his friends and tells them about the addition to their group. Charlie and Nuno like the idea but Brad says, "Can he keep up?" Instead of answering, Max turns his back.

It's a pretty day, perfect for riding, and days like this are one of the things that makes being a biker in Southern California worthwhile. Brad leads, as he always insists, and decides to ride over twisty Little Tujunga Canyon.

When they get there, however, Brad keeps taking the turns either too wide or too slow. It's embarrassing. Not only to him but to his three friends who were foolish enough to allow him to lead.

He turns on the music on his bike hoping it'll take everyone's mind off of his faulty riding. It doesn't work but after only a couple of miles, he comes up with the excuse that he must be overtired from last night. He turns up the music.

Another thing that's bothering Brad is that the stranger never falters, a fact that makes him wish he would just go away. Missteps keep plaguing Brad and he decides they need to pull over as soon as possible, which means a sit-down at The Big Oaks on Bouquet Canyon.

When they get there, Charlie asks, "Why're we stopping here?"

"Oh, figured you guys needed a rest. Besides, I had a long night, know what I mean?" Out the corner of his eye, he looks at the stranger to see if he's impressed. He isn't. "Anyways, let's just get a beer."

Sitting outside, Brad does get an imported beer but the other four get sodas and lemonade. Brad immediately begins boasting about the superiority of his bike, his income, his prowess with women and everything else. But it's like he's talking to only the wind, which is a bit unsettling to him. He even tries to flirt with the waitress but she ignores him as well.

Normally, his three friends would put up with him but today, as you may expect, they're only curious about their new riding companion, who sits like a breathing statue. The problem is that Brad is talking nonstop and none of them can get a word in. Finally, when Brad takes a drink of his beer, Max is able to ask the stranger his name.

"Willmont."

"Willmont?"

"Yeah."

"Last name?"

"Smith. Willmont Absaroka Smith."

Brad chortles. "How'd ya get a name like that?"

"Daddy was William, granddaddy was Montgomery."

"And Ass-uh-broker?"

"Momma was born in the Absaroka Mountains. Montana."

Brad scoffs. Max is annoyed with him but is more interested in Willmont. "So what do you do?"

"Nothing. Retired recently."

"What did you do."

"One year Army, three years Rangers, eleven years CIA."

Brad pops up again. "CIA?"

"Yes."

"Why'd you quit?"

Like Max, Willmont is a keen observer, though skilled in a different way, and he finally puts his full attention on Brad. He stares at Brad with an inexplicable look, his mental machinations eluding even Max. Charlie and Nuno watch and wait, too.

The silence grows and the air becomes heavy and uneasy. Willmont keeps staring at Brad, who's flicking his eyes back and forth. He finally says, "Got tired of killing people."

A tremble goes through Brad. "Killing people?"

"Yes."

"You serious?"

"Yes."

Brad nervously half-smiles. "The CIA kills people?"

"Much of what they do."

"So what'd you do? Like wipe out villages and stuff?"

"No."

Brad can't help himself. "What then?"

"Individuals antipathetic to the interests of the United States."

"So you'd get a photo from some guy in a cafe and and go out and kill him?"

"Pretty much."

Brad's eyes are darting around and he's trying to smile, hoping it's all a joke, but Willmont continues to calmly look at him. The others are also quiet.

Finally, Nuno speaks up. "My dad was in the army. Got wounded in Desert Storm. Still has a limp."

Willmont looks at Nuno. "Give him my best and make sure you always take care of him."

Nuno nods.

The five men slowly sip their drinks. Charlie nonplussed, Nuno thinking about his dad, Max still observing Willmont, Brad flashing from anxiety to fear.

The waitress comes over and serves another round of drinks, saving her smile for when she gives Willmont his lemonade. He smiles and nods once, "Thank you, darling."

"Sure thing, big fella."

The five become silent again and after a few minutes, Brad speaks up. "How many?"

Willmont takes a slow drink of lemonade and looks at him, still with an unanalyzable gaze. He waits. "All together or just the CIA?"

"Just with the CIA."

"Thirty-three."

"One at a time?"

"Mostly."

Brad is visibly shaking. He'd never before met anyone like Willmont, never even thought that anyone like him could exist outside of a movie. After some minutes, he comes out of his stupor. "How? Like with a sniper rifle?"

"Knife."

"Why?"

"Quick and quiet."

"So you just stab 'em?"

Willmont watches a sparrow light on the ground then fly away. "Left hand over the mouth, slice through the larynx then all four jugulars."

"I thought there was just one jugular."

Willmont doesn't answer. In a sort of perverted way, Charlie finds this fascinating. "How'd you learn to do that?"

"First dolls then cadavers."

Again the men fall silent. Willmont continues looking at Brad, who's trying to think of a way out. Something, anything, that will change the subject, but he can't. Finally, he says, "But how'd they know you killed the guy? They just take your word for it?"

"Cut their head off and bring it back."

"How?"

138

"A short tree trimming saw. Deep teeth."

"But what about all the blood?"

"One reason you cut the jugulars first."

The air is still. Constrictive. Brad pauses, thinking. "How long does it take."

Willmont, still staring at Brad, pauses as well then takes a long breath. "To kill 'em or cut the head off?"

"Both, I guess."

"Cutting and blood letting takes three or four minutes. A coupla three with the sawing."

Nuno stares at his glass trying to relate what Willmont was saying with the stories he'd heard from his father. Max continues to observe and now Charlie is, too. Brad's mind is reeling. He asks, "So how'd you get the head back?"

"A bag."

"What kind?"

"The kind ya carry a soccer ball in. That way if people see ya, they don't think nothing of it."

Charlie asks, "Wouldn't it start to smell after a while?"

"Ya cover it with lime."

Everyone falls silent for another minute. Brad asks him, "Ever kill any kids?"

"No."

"Women?"

"Two."

"Why?"

"They was antipathetic to the interests of the United States."

———❧———

The five men finish their drinks, mount up and again, Brad takes the lead. Following is Nuno then Charlie who are each lost in his own thoughts. Next is Max and though he's lost in his own thoughts as well, he's taking an unexpected comfort knowing that Willmont is behind him.

Brad is shaking like the last leaf clinging to a branch at the end of autumn, mostly because Willmont represents something he can't come to terms with. It becomes a speed-up-a-little-slow-down-a-lot type of ride.

They're still on Bouquet Canyon and after a few minutes, Willmont slows down until there's a good hundred yards between him and Max, then speeds up and takes the curves as is his wont. Max notices this and follows suit, then Charlie and Nuno.

This confuses Brad and he ends up figuring that the reason must be that he's taking the curves too fast and the other four catch up only when he slows down on the straightaways, which is the exact opposite of how it really is.

After turning left onto Spunky Canyon, Brad speeds up to ninety on the first straightaway but when they come to the curves, he has become so bereft of any kind of canyon expertise that the other four can't slow down enough to make any space. They end up looking like underfed cattle on a cattle drive.

They finally make it to the Rock Inn, go inside and sit at an empty table. Brad, somewhat back to himself again, begins to bluster about his expertise with everything but not as loudly or with as much certainty as before.

Luckily, a rocking-loud three-piece band soon starts up, and for the next forty-five minutes, the five men sit and listen. When the band takes a break, Charlie turns to Willmont. "So thirty-three in eleven years. What'd you do in your off time?"

"Women and drugs at first."

Brad smiles. "Were they CIA women?"

"No."

After some silence, Nuno says, "My dad told me about them. Some were hookers but others were just local women with nothing else to do. Said he never felt right about taking advantage of them, but he did now and then."

"Yeah, that's pretty much the way it was for me, too."

Max asks, "Were you just in one place all the time?"

"I's all over."

Charlie asks, "So how'd you find someone to get drugs from when you got to a new place?"

"CIA took care of that."

"The CIA gave you drugs?" Nuno asks.

"Yeah."

"What kind?"

"Any kind ya want. Some of 'em were special made for certain things."

140

Brad calls the waitress over for another round. He slaps her butt and gets a cold stare. Max flares his nostrils in disgust.

Charlie asks, "What kinds of certain things?"

"Stay awake for a week, mutilate bodies like a machine, photographic memory, nonstop sex. Whatever ya want."

Brad, thinking this is the opening for something he can relate to, says, "Nonstop sex? That sounds like fun."

Again, Willmont looks at Brad like he was a broken down rag doll. "It ain't."

"Why?"

"Go at it for days and alls you can remember is that ya had sex for days. Don't remember any enjoyment or details or who you was with."

"So you spent like eight or nine months a year for eleven years getting high and fucking?"

"No."

"What then?" Charlie asks.

"I quit taking the ones from the CIA after half a year. Felt like a guinea pig, so I went back to just smoking pot. Eventually quit that, too. Got my head on straight."

Max asks, "Then what'd you do?"

"Read books and worked out."

———

If it was awkward inside, it's more so once the men get outside, what with them just standing next to their bikes not saying anything. But it doesn't take long before Brad hears some other bikers talking about a new paint job, so he goes over and brags about his.

The other four men continue standing around, Charlie and Nuno smoking cigarettes, Max and Willmont looking around, taking in the scene. When Brad turns his back to them, Max walks over to his bike and turns the gas lever to "off."

After the other bikers have successfully walked away, one by one, Brad comes back and says they should mount up. They take off on Elizabeth Lake Road going east and back home, but a quarter mile later, Brad's bike sputters once then dies. He has no clue why so he paces and mumbles to himself, cursing his mechanic. The others commiserate with his bad luck and say they'll stay with him and ride back with the tow truck.

But Brad doesn't care about that because the real bothersome thing is that his embarrassment is growing by the second. He finally says, "Why don't you guys just go on. Don't wanna ruin a good day of riding for you."

The other four take off going west, Max leading.

———◦———

Ten miles later, they turn left onto Pine Canyon and take the curves at a good pace, but not crazy fast, being that much of the road is covered with a fair amount of gravel and small branches. They ride down the Ridge Route, turn left on Lancaster Road and when they get to Interstate 5, head north to Gorman where they top off their tanks.

Five minutes later, they hit Lockwood Valley Road at a good clip, thoughts focussed. When they get to Highway 33, Max pulls into a turnout.

As you may expect, there's a fair amount of excitement among the four riders. And though Max has yet to see Willmont smile, he notices that he is more content.

He takes in the pretty blue sky that's dotted with a small cloud here and there, and several times breathes in the dry mountain air. Willmont does the same while Charlie and Nuno smoke cigarettes and talk about how much fun that stretch of road was.

Max turns to his friends and says, "Monday's a holiday, right?" Charlie and Nuno nod. "Well, today's Saturday. What do you say we ride north to the 166 then head west? Maybe have lunch at the Burger Barn in New Cuyama and spend the night in Santa Maria."

Charlie says, "Sounds good but if we don't turn left, we'll miss all those twisties. Is the Burger Barn a good place?"

"Oh yeah. But then, I've been there only once. There're no twisties up there but there's a side road off the 166 that has some good ones. Besides, we'll get out of our neighborhood, go to some place new."

Nuno asks, "Is it pretty?"

"If you like scrublands and dust. It's about as close to the middle of nowhere as you can get. Until you get into the mountains anyway. But like I said, we'll be someplace new."

Charlie and Nuno think it's a good idea. Willmont is up for anything.

———◦———

Highway 33 going north is in decent shape and pretty much straight, and because there's almost no other traffic, they cover the twenty miles in well under fifteen minutes, make a left on Highway 166, and five minutes later pull over at the Burger Barn.

While eating, Charlie, harboring a million questions, asks Willmont, "What about retribution? I mean, there have to be some people who want you dead."

"Might happen sooner or later."

"Aren't you worried?"

"Nah. If I get killed, I'll be dead is all. I deserve it. Ain't got no family to worry about."

Nuno asks, "Sleep with a gun?"

"Yeah. And a knife."

"So you should be okay."

"'Fraid not. If some other guy like me wants me dead, I'll be dead. Nothing I can do about it."

Max asks, "How many are there? You know, in your former line of work. In the whole world."

"Well, there's a lot of people who'd kill for the money but they's easy to spot and avoid. But if yer asking how many're skilled at it, I'd say a coupla three hundred, give or take."

"Are most of them independent?"

"No. Most of 'em work for some agency. There's some independents, though."

The men fall silent again and dive into their lunches, which is understandable because the burgers are big, juicy and tasty, and the fries have the right amount of crunch.

When they finish eating, Max says, "Well, if we're going to make Santa Maria before sunset, we'd better be getting on."

———— ∿ ————

There's a fair amount of traffic on the 166 so the riders are going the speed limit but it's not frustrating because the weather is ideal and once they get into the low mountains, the views are pretty darn good.

Max had been up there just once before, about ten years before, with his younger brother. They were on sport bikes at the time, newly bought, and he remembers the name of a road that begins with the letter T. He keeps an eye out for it and about forty miles later, turns left.

Most of Tepusquet Road isn't wide enough for a center line, and there are cracks here and there, some filled with tar snakes, but there's no traffic at all, which suits everyone.

After riding for an hour on straight roads, however, the first twisty they come to is a surprise and almost results in a four-bike accident. The second one is a bit smoother, but the ones after that have the four riders in perfect form, scraping pegs in rhythmic sequence: shhhing-shhhing-shing-shhhing.

Once the road straightens out, they stop to take in the view, which isn't magnificent but welcomed nonetheless. Max had been right about getting out of their neighborhood and all four of them feel much better about everything.

When they get toward the end of Tepusquet, they ride through thriving vineyards and vibrant fields of alfalfa and soy bean. At the 101 Freeway, Max turns north and stops at the Motel 6 on the north side of Santa Maria. All in all, it wasn't the greatest of rides but it was a rush of freedom to be away from their comfort roads.

———◦———

As Motel 6s go, this is one of the nicer ones with two-story wings on three sides of a pool. Thinking that because Willmont is unemployed and might be low on money, both Charlie and Nuno offer to share a room with him, but he declines saying his finances are just fine. Max, Charlie and Nuno get three rooms next to each other on the same side as the office, while Willmont's is at the end of the opposite wing.

After unloading, Max goes to a liquor store and buys two six-packs. The four then ride west as far as they can on Main Street, park their bikes and walk to a deserted beach. For a short while they all stare at the endless Pacific, letting the cool ocean breezes flow through their hair.

Soon, they take off their boots and socks, roll up their jeans and wade into the blue waters. The mood is a superior one and they get into some good-natured horseplay. Eventually, they're soaked from top to bottom.

Getting back to the beach, they sit on the warm sand and drink. There's no conversation, really, but Max notices that for the first time Willmont is smiling.

After the first round of beers, Charlie and Nuno begin with the jokes and at one point Willmont laughs out loud, uncontrollably, as if it's something he hadn't done for a decade.

They quiet down and become contemplative as they watch the sun slowly get bigger and change colors and disappear into the ocean. Max looks at Willmont. "What's the scene with your family?"

Willmont closes his eyes, barely breathing. "It was about fifteen years ago. Three guys came into a diner and started shooting up the place. Momma and daddy was there having dinner and my daddy shot and killed one. Another one got wounded. Might have been my daddy that did it, maybe not, don't know. Last guy killed momma and daddy before somebody killed him. My daddy and some others saved a lot of lives that day.

"Grandparents on both sides died some years before that. What used to be my sister is somewheres up north convinced that guns're evil and calling for all of 'em to be taken away and all soldiers called home to be monitored with drugs and then everybody'll be singing Kumbaya and the world will be at peace."

He digs shallow holes in the sand with a small stick. "When I's home for the funeral, it didn't bother me when she screamed that I's a murderer 'cause that's what I am, but when she spit on my daddy's face, I figured she ain't no family of mine no more."

"That's messed up."

"Yeah. But it's for the better 'cause I don't have no one to worry about no more."

"How'd you get started in all this?"

"Well, I's in the Army, but not much was going on where I was and it was pretty boring so I joined the Rangers and got sent to Afghanistan. Lots of small battles and killed some, got credit for 'em but don't know how many exactly."

He looks up at the darkening sky. A cool puff of air blows across their faces. "One afternoon, we was sweeping a small settlement and seven of us got ambushed in what used to be a store of some kind.

"There's eleven of 'em and they was hiding in there waiting fer us. One of 'em tried to set off an IED but it didn't blow and that was pure luck. We killed all of 'em but they wounded two of ours.

"I's helping one of the wounded get out, both his legs had taken two bullets, when we got ambushed by another dozen or so. The first one bull-rushed me and we fought a bit. I's able to get my knife out and stab him under the ribs. First time I killed up close.

"A sniper took out the next guy and he kept the rest of 'em at bay for a coupla hours till backup came."

Willmont looks out at the dark ocean, the light crashing waves like a slow funeral march. "The thing is, when that guy bull-rushed me, I fell back on my buddy and crushed both his legs. He's living in a wheelchair now and part of that was me doing it."

He looks down at his hands, closes then opens them. "Met the sniper a few days later and we hit it off. He's one tough son of a gun, tell ya what. I's always pretty good with a rifle so he helped me get into the program."

He shakes his head once, his eyes glazed over with remembrance. "That Ranger Sniper Program is tough, real tough, but I got through it and got real good but not as good as some of 'em. I's dead-on up to three hundred yards but some of them guys … shit. I came to believe they could hit a running squirrel from five miles out. I wasn't the best but I had my uses.

"Did that for a couple of years and, to be honest, most of the time it was boring as hell, just lying there looking through a scope. And when I killed someone there was no action to it, so that was getting me down, too. Happens a lot."

He takes a big breath and looks at the sand between his legs. "Anyways, one day a CIA guy comes up and asks if I wanna go work for them. I's looking for anything different so I signed right up. Trained for six months and the next day went on my first kill. It was easy, satisfying almost, 'cause I felt special. Elite-like.

"By then I wasn't thinking about why I's killing, just that I was. And I's real good at it, too. Never failed a mission."

Willmont looks back out at the dark ocean. The impossible distance, the stars struggling to be seen, the small but implacable waves, sounds muffled by the wet air. The other three look at Willmont's silhouette.

After a while, he says, "Tell ya one thing, though. I sure could use some dinner."

———

After dinner, they walk to a local watering hole and begin drinking again. And talking and joking around and Willmont seems to be having the best time. Eventually, they quiet down and Max asks him, "So with all that past behind you, what're your plans?"

"Oh, don't know, really. Figure to ride for a while, always wanted to do that, maybe see the country."

"That's gonna cost a lot," Charlie says.

"Yeah. But I have so much money I don't know what to do with it."

Nuno asks, "The CIA pays that well?"

Willmont laughs out loud and beer spurts out his nose. "No. I mean, the pay's okay but most of what I have I stole."

Max says, "Oh great. Not only are we riding with an assassin, we're drinking with an international thief!"

Willmont smiles wide and Max thinks how good it is to see that. "So was it like a second job? Moonlighting?"

"Just part of the work. See some jewelry, find some cash, ya just grab it. Sometimes ya get bad intel and end up in a place where there ain't nobody, maybe a servant or two, so ya sneak in and steal whatever's there that ya can carry."

Charlie asks, "So how much do you have?"

"A million. Maybe two."

"Damn!"

Around ten o'clock, the place fills up and is rocking hard. And man, are they having fun. Good natured rabble-rousing and buying drinks for other patrons and dancing, including Willmont who moves like a drunk flamingo. It endears him to the ladies and they each take their turn with him. After midnight, the four men head back to their rooms.

———⁓———

Around eight o'clock the following morning, Max, Charlie, and Nuno are up and about. They talk a bit about where to ride next but can't come to a decision. However, breakfast and coffee for their slight hangovers are definitely on their minds and as the minutes pass, they're hoping Willmont will show up but he doesn't. None of them want to knock on his door, for some reason thinking he needs his sleep.

There's no restaurant at the Motel 6, but next door is a Holiday Inn that has one. Before walking there, Charlie leaves a come-join-us note on Willmont's bike. Max has an uneasy feeling but can't figure out why.

Uneasiness keeps creeping into Max's thoughts so just before ordering, he says, "I don't know, man, something isn't right. I'm gonna go back and get Willmont." Charlie and Nuno tag along.

Max knocks then pounds on Willmont's door. Not a sound. He waits then pounds some more.

Nuno says, "He's just dead asleep. Drank too much." Max doesn't respond.

Charlie looks at Max long and hard. "What, man?"

"Don't know. Something's wrong. Gonna get the manager."

The manager, a middle-aged, disheveled man, unlocks the door, slowly opens it and stands in the doorway, squinting his eyes to adjust them to the darkness. He freezes. After some seconds, he slowly closes the door, locks it, walks away, vomits, then pulls out his phone.

Soon, four police cars with their lights flashing and an EMT van are in front of Willmont's room. People stand in small groups, quietly talking to one another. Cross their arms then uncross them. The motel manager nervously walks here and there. The police question the three friends. Write down their words.

For the rest of the day, Max, Charlie and Nuno mill about, sit on the curb, sometimes shake their heads. Half-heartedly stare. The air is still and heavy like the inside of an abandoned house on a long summer day. The sun grows big and slowly disappears, the sky turns from pale yellow and orange to indigo.

In the gloaming, two paramedics roll out a gurney with a body bag on it. The sheet underneath is scattered with blood spots. Next, a doctor walks out, then a female paramedic carrying a thick canvas bag, inside of which is something the size of a soccer ball.

END

FINDING JANEY
(THE PROMISE)

The sky and the earth,
The night and the light,
The heat and the cold,
The rain and the drought;
Those are my demigods.

But the road,
The road is my mistress.
Devious and open,
Harsh and nurturing,
She seduces me with love
And dares me with death
In equal measure.

Like any good woman.

I've known women, more than my share. Married three of them and for different reasons became bereft of each. With Carla, it was her drinking. With Wanda it was drugs. With Belinda, it was both, but that time those two demons were my own as well.

All women are good, I do believe, and all women are part harpy, too. The telling thing is the balance between the two. The ones who are almost all on the good side will understand and forgive your faults, but then you end up feeling guilty for not being good enough for them.

The ones who are mostly harpy will come right out and point out all your faults, past and present, making your life miserable.

Over the years, I've known only a handful who had that balance just right and how fine it was to be around them. The conversations, the laughing, the sex, all of it damn good.

The memories of those women, thankfully, are the ones that have stayed with me, given me an occasional smile. But of all of them, the one I most enjoy remembering, the one I seem to always think about, is you, Janey.

Three months ago I was on this old Shovelhead riding into Joplin through one of those this-don't-ever-happen-this-time-of-year thunderstorms, reminiscing about the two times we went there.

The first was when we met that old-timer we bought a couple of beers for. He'd been telling us stories for an hour or so when he said he wanted to buy us a steak dinner, but we didn't want him to because he looked a little down on his luck and we didn't want him to spend his money on two strangers.

But he insisted so we said okay and it turned out he was a multi-millionaire rancher who liked to walk the streets now and again thinking about the good old days when he was a "cherub-faced ranch hand."

But the second time in Joplin? Now that was wild.

We were in this big bar that was loud and packed full, minding our own business and talking about anything and everything. Getting excited about it all, too. Then one of us would make a stupid pun or joke and we'd laugh and almost fall off our chairs, then order another beer. Nothing but a run-o-the-mill night for us, right?

Anyway, I noticed three guys checking you out, which wasn't unusual by any means of measure, but there was one in particular that I reckoned had bad intentions.

I wasn't worried about anything bad happening to you because I'd never allow that. Besides, you never had a problem with taking care of yourself. No, the real problem was that I had to pee real bad but didn't want to leave you all alone, so I kept sitting there and holding it in.

After a while, that depraved slime came over, his two minions in tow, put his hand on your shoulder and said you ought to go with them so you could find out what a real good time was. I looked at him square and said that wasn't going to happen.

He turned to me and with this plastic smile on his face told me about how his buddies and him had some sort of black belts and did I really think I could take on all three of them. I said I doubt I could but on the way down I'd be sure to mess him up so bad he wouldn't ever have any children. That backed him off for a while, but it took you to send him away for good.

We went back to our conversation like nothing happened but he kept standing at the bar staring at you all lascivious like. Well, it soon got to the point where I couldn't hold in the pee any longer, so I excused myself and went to the bathroom.

Coming back, just like I figured it, that guy was coming on to you real fast. I was still down the hallway so you couldn't see me, but I heard you talking to him real loud so everybody in the place could hear.

The last thing you said was, "My old man does me three times a night with a dick the size of a giant redwood. Now tell me again, what's so special about you?" I swear, I doubled over from laughing so hard. It was the only time I ever heard you tell a lie, Janey, and I loved you for it. Still do.

———

Another thing I wanted to tell you was that I rode Moki Dugway again. Remember when we did that? We'd camped the night before in Bear's Ears, got up with the sun and figured we'd ride south on the Moki and get a big chorizo omelet in Mexican Hat. Other than being a little on the cool side, it was a fine day and we were feeling as content as we could feel.

When we got up to that one lookout, we stopped and took in the view of the Valley of the Gods for a long time. It was one of those times when we didn't say a word because we both knew we had the exact same thoughts.

It was a while before we got back on the bike and when the road started going down, we slipped and slid a little here and there but the tires would always grab hold.

Then, not a half mile later, the dirt road gave way and we started sliding down and there was no way to stop. I kept us upright for a ways but got to the point where we had no choice but to jump off. The bike kept going, hit a small boulder and went flying over the side, doing somersaults for hundreds of feet.

We weren't hurt and that was sheer luck. We walked over to the cliffside and again stood for the longest time, silent and just looking. First at the bike then at the purple shadows in the hazy distance cleaving their way into the sky where a lone cloud sat like an angel of fate.

After a while, you said with that silky voice of yours, "Within every good experience is the promise for more; within every bad experience is the promise for better times."

Now, I've never known anyone else who could have come up with a fine philosophy like that but you, Janey. Especially right after our bike got mangled and everything we owned was strewn across the mountainside. My, oh my.

The way we looked at it, we didn't ride on roads, we rode on the earth itself. And when we made love, well, there were times we did that right on the earth, too. We were never at a loss for words and every experience was recounted with philosophy and humor. We had no one but ourselves and that was everything.

Remember when we first met in that bar outside of Denver? We'd each just gotten some money from an inheritance and were looking for adventure.

We hit it right off, laid together that night and the next morning, without saying a word about any plans, got a big down sleeping bag, wrapped all our things in it, strapped it on the back of my old Panhead and took off.

For three years we rode. We were young and money-foolish, I guess, but looking back, I can honestly say it was the right thing to do.

We went everywhere, seems like. Even up to Alaska and I remember getting caught in that thunderstorm and burying ourselves into that sleeping bag after we'd thrown it under an outcropping of rock and when we woke up at sunrise – damn the air was so still and crisp! – we saw that a family of porcupines had joined us.

152

That time we said goodbye is the only sad memory I have. Your mom and my dad had just passed so we each had to go back home to sort out things. We were standing there waiting for the bus to take you back to Virginia, the Panhead pointing toward California, holding each other, not saying a word, not wanting to let go. Crying. Felt like a lifetime.

We both thought we'd see each other again but we never did. Life works out like that sometimes, doesn't it? Just before you stepped on that bus is when I made my promise to you, Janey. I promised that it didn't matter where you were or how long it had been, someday I'd find you.

At first, we kept in touch every day but then I fell in with a nurse and by the time we broke up you'd fallen in with that lawyer fellow, so our letters changed to read like we were just good friends.

By the time you broke up with him, I'd met another nurse and by the time we broke up, you'd started with that jeweler guy. And it kept going on like that. The letters became less and less frequent.

I guess it was my fault we finally fell out of touch for good. It was my third marriage and that's when I started with the hard stuff. Hell, I was out of touch with everyone and everything except my own demons.

When I finally dried out, I found out that my wife had burned all your letters and thrown out everything that was from you or about you. She was a mean woman.

It wasn't until years and years later with my three sons grown up and married and me a grandpa seven times over and a great grandpa seventeen times, that I started looking for you. Came up with nothing. Didn't have much at the time and most of what I didn't have was money, so I got my finances together and hired a private investigator.

He found you. You'd been living in New Jersey and were listed among the dead from hurricane Sandy. He also found your daughter, Sadie. I called her immediately and right away she knew who I was because you'd told her all about our times together. That just warmed my heart. She had to do most of the talking because I was choked up.

But it was mostly Sadie's voice that sent me back down my memories. It sounded so much like yours. At one point, I had her recite what you said that morning decades ago on Moki Dugway: Within every good experience is the promise for more; within every bad experience is the promise for better times. I closed my eyes and I could see us, clear as a spring day, arms wrapped around each other, standing on that cliffside.

The very next day, I climbed on this old Shovelhead and rode across the country to see her. I have to say it, Janey, you did a fine job of being a mother. When Sadie smiled I could see your light in her eyes and cheeks.

Sadie also lost everything in that hurricane and she told me everything she had of yours was lost or destroyed, too, including my letters. So there was nothing left, not one thing in the world that connected us.

But I made that promise, that promise that someday I'd find you. Now, I've broken a lot of promises in my life, I know that, and I feel remorse for all of them. But I never broke a promise to you, Janey, and that's why I'm roaming all over, going to every place we went to, trying to find something, anything, that would connect us back up. And my last chance to find that something is right here in Wyoming.

———

Predicting weather is not part of my expertise and if there's one thing that following the advice of weathermen will teach you, is that it's not part of anyone else's expertise either.

It was early spring and we were in Wyoming, and late one morning, we saddled up to just ride wherever. I was wearing a t-shirt, jeans and boots but you were on the back in nothing but flip-flops, that flimsy blue halter-top and those short shorts, neither of which covered up much, which was fine by me. The temperature was in the mid-70s and there wasn't much of a wind so it was okay, comfortable even.

Then that freezing storm came out of nowhere, hitting us like Thor's hammer. We were lost and there was no place where we could hide from the wind and the rain and the freezing air. Not even an abandoned building or some rocks or trees.

Damn, I've never been so cold. But we kept riding and praying and it got to the point where I could barely move. Honestly, I don't know how you survived, Janey, dressed like you were.

After a while, I saw a place a mile or so up ahead and as we got closer, I could see it was an old and rundown roadside motel. I pulled in and the owner, an older German woman, Helen, came running out saying, "Oh Lord, oh Lord" over and over.

She had to actually pry you off the bike. Then she took you into the first motel room, put you in the bathtub and turned on the cold water. Even put in some ice cubes so you wouldn't go into shock.

I hated to see you like that, Janey, so cold you weren't even shaking.

154

Helen did a good job of warming you back up but it took a long time. It wasn't until the third day that you were talking and had mostly come around. I was so grateful I didn't know what to say or how to act.

Helen kept on taking real good care of us after that – man, could she cook or what! – and she loved it when we called her Mom. We stayed there through spring fixing up the place. I did the carpentry and some plumbing, and you and Helen did the painting and decorating. The place looked real fine after we finished, didn't it?

The time we spent there was something else. Going for day rides two or three times a week. Going for walks. Laughing and dreaming. We were in love before that, but that's when we first felt that love through and through.

There was one place that became our favorite. It was a few minute's walk down the road then up a footpath about a hundred yards. There was a tree there, a chalk maple, and what a chalk maple was doing in Wyoming we never figured out, but there it was. Looked to be not that old but it was big enough with enough leaves to cast a nice shadow.

It was in the middle of a small, scratchy area scattered with several large rocks, but the ground around it was soft and there was a patch of grass. We would put our sleeping bag on it and lie there forever it seemed like, much of the time looking up through the leaves and to the sky, your head on my shoulder and my arm around yours.

It was a day or two before we said goodbye to Helen when we went to lie under that tree for the last time. I got out my knife and carved our initials into the trunk. You laughed that sweet giggle-laugh of yours and said that's something teenagers do and we're not teenagers anymore. I said we weren't that many years removed from it and, besides, I wanted us to be forever and this was the way to do it.

When I was done, you put your arms around my neck, looked up at me with those infinite eyes and gave me, gave us, the sweetest kiss.

———— ✧ ————

I'm old now. Broken down. Tired. Walk slow, don't eat much or talk much. Can't sit or lie too long in one position, either. And this old Shovelhead I'm on, I guess you could say it's in the same condition. It needs fixing up, a lot of fixing up, but I've prayed it'll get me to you, Janey, and I know it will. So I keep riding, both the bike and me getting more broken down by the mile.

Up till yesterday, I'd spent a whole month in Wyoming, going up every side road I came across, but couldn't find that motel or that tree. But I knew I had to. I had to keep my promise and find you, Janey.

And yesterday was when it happened. I was riding along thinking about our good times and didn't know I was on the right road till I was passing by that old place. Barely recognized it.

I turned around and rode back and, hell, it's a skeleton of what it once was, so bereft of everything that rats don't even live there. Even that bathtub where Helen saved your life is long gone. All the paint's peeled off, too.

I walked to the end of the building, looked to the right and, sure enough, that chalk maple was still there, about a dozen feet taller than it was back then, but it looked like it didn't have much more life in it than me.

It was too far to walk so I rode the bike up that footpath, which was barely visible, got off and looked and looked but the tree was barren of initials. Looked all up and down, even walked all around it, but nothing.

I stood there for the longest time and thought about us. What we did and what we could have done and would have. Didn't even know I was crying until the sun broke through some branches and slapped me back to the present.

I'd come as far as I could, Janey. Couldn't think of anywhere else to go and I guess that old Shovelhead knew it, too, because it wouldn't start. We'd both come to our end. I put it back on its kickstand, got off and took one more long look all up and down that tree. Finally I lay down on that patch of grass and fell asleep.

———❧———

I slept right through the afternoon and all through the night. When the morning sun woke me up, I felt nothing, Janey, nothing at all. All the pains and aches were gone and I wasn't even numb or cold or hot. It was like all of me had somehow left.

I managed to rub the sleep out of my eyes, looked up, and there they were. Our initials. The bark had grown over them and the sun was at just the right angle to cast a light shadow.

JJ
&
Janey
Forever

I smiled. I could see those shadows, our shadows, for just three minutes, but it was an eternity, an eternity of bliss. And when they were gone, I continued smiling and closed my eyes for the last time. I kept my promise and found you, Janey. I finally found you.

END

FALLING IN LOVE

An excellent day for riding a motorcycle. Actually, it's pretty darn hot but with cruising at seventy to ninety miles-per-hour on a superslab, it's not a chore to bear.

Here in Eastern Colorado, the land is about as flat as flat can get, but when you have the Rockies rising up behind you, you're gifted with an expanse that you can fill with whatever you want. And I'm filling it up with a big ol' smile.

A year or so ago, my parents opened a diner in West Virginia on Highway 33 just north of Riverton called Good Folks Good Times. I've yet to see the place but I know the food has to be good, real good, because my mom is a helluva cook.

My dad is, too, but only with red meat and chicken. I mean, he's the complete opposite of a vegetarian. In fact, I don't think he could tell the difference between a spoonful of tofu and a spinach leaf.

So the plan is to continue east for four or five days, hang with my parents for a while, then on the way back home, spend a coupla-three-or-four days visiting my friend, Kaylee, in Lexington. Sweet gal. Lives alone. Real Pretty. Dedicated painter.

As I'm mulling this over, I start to think about stopping at Kaylee's first then my parent's. And the more I think about it, the more I'm liking the idea. I don't have a specific time to be at my parent's place, so why not?

I call Kaylee. She answers on the second ring. "Hold on." I'm figuring to wait a good two minutes while she washes the paint off her hands. It's a standard thing with her. Three minutes later she's back. "Hey, stud, what's up?" Stud. Hah!

I tell her where I am and that I'm wondering if she'll be around for a while in three or four days, that I'd like to hang out.

She's full of enthusiasm. "Gawd, that'd be great! Been painting so much that I haven't seen anyone but the neighbors for months."

"Great! I'll call ya when I'm a day away."

She assumes a mock-bossy tone. "Hold on, Buster. Just to be clear, you're gonna take me out to lunch and dinner every day and I'm not talking about Taco Bell."

I chuckle once then agree. Knowing Kaylee, it's a fantastic deal.

———~———

Four days later, I roll onto the driveway of Kaylee's little one-bedroom place. I no sooner remove my helmet than she's running out to greet me in her inimitable way, meaning a wrap-around hug and endless kisses, the last of which is long and deep. Tell ya what, that woman is something else.

We've known each other for some years now, six to be exact, so the preamble to the heated action is over before a minute passes. You could barely call it foreplay. I mean, it's unbelievable how fast we get off all our clothes.

An hour later, we're lying on her bed getting our breaths back and the sweat is starting to dry when she says, "So what ya got planned?"

I look at her. "Kaylee, I'm a guy. All I can think of is you and I fucking our brains out."

She giggles. "Well, there's this Blues Festival tonight I want to go to. And I don't wanna be sitting on the grass in the back; I want to be up front in the VIP section. It's forty bucks a ticket."

I nod. "Okay."

"And I wanna have dinner at this new cafe close to there. It's pretty upscale so it might be expensive but it's cute and seems friendly."

I nod again. "Okay."

"And afterwards, I wanna take one of those horse-drawn carriages around downtown. See all those little Disneyland-like lights lighting everything up."

Looking at a three-hundred dollar night at least, I nod for the third time. "Okay."

She snuggles up to me with her head on my shoulder. There are some hours before the Blues Festival so we fall asleep. We wake up an hour or so later and within a minute we're going at it again like a couple of eighteen-year-olds. I've said it before and I'll say it again: that Kaylee is something else.

———

We finished showering and are just starting to dress, eager to enjoy a night on the town, when Kaylee says, "It's warm out. Let's take your bike." No objection from me.

Now, it's true that Kaylee is a painter, a really fine one, and her style is a little on the, I don't know, traditional side. "Raphael with a dash of Renoir" is the way she puts it.

But damn, despite that, does she know how to dress like the ultimate biker chick! Long and wavy blond hair tied back, black and blood-red headband, I-dare-ya sunglasses, black boots, tight-assed jeans, and a show-off top. And trust me, she has way more than a little to show off. Plus, she has that attitude, that biker chick attitude, that just turns me and the rest of us on.

It's only five miles to the cafe but the late afternoon Friday traffic makes it a heat-filled, forty-five minute, not-much-fun ride. We get to the new, upscale and "might be expensive" cafe and, like Kaylee said, it is a cute place and darn friendly.

I say that because even though we're dressed like bikers, the maitre d' is cordial as are the rest of the staff. But then, that has become the usual in the past I-don't-know-how-many years. I mean, people dress all sorts of ways these days. Let's face it, the days of required tuxedos for the men and gowns for the women are long gone.

We get a quiet table in a corner next to a window. When I open the menu, I think to myself, "Might be expensive? Good Lord!" But for Kaylee's sake, I go with it. It's a six-course meal and, to be honest, it's rather tasty. After dessert, I'm perfectly full and totally satisfied. I'm not saying it was worth it, but in a way I guess it was.

I get the bill. Two dinners and wine (I drank water) come to $225. Add to it a tip – I tip well – and we walk out of there with my bank account $325 lighter. And I remember why it is I visit Kaylee for only a couple or three days once or twice a year.

The Blues Festival is only two blocks away so we leave the bike in the cafe's parking lot and walk there. There aren't many VIP tickets left so the price has gone from forty to sixty dollars each. Well, Kaylee is Kaylee and she always gets what she wants, so I pony up the bankcard again.

Tonight is the first night of the festival and the three bands are damn good, especially the last one, Calloway's Wayward Sons. But the thrill cranks up several notches when Derek Trucks and his wife, Susan, walk onto the stage and sit in with them. Tell ya what, those last three songs alone make the 120 dollars for tickets and the thirty bucks for beer worth it.

We're walking back to my bike and I'm hoping Kaylee has forgotten about that horse-pulled carriage ride, what with the $475 I've already spent. I don't say anything, neither does she. But then I start to feel guilty, and though I'm not lying, I feel like I am, so I bring it up.

Kaylee stops and gazes into my eyes with her enduring sweetness. "I'm tired. Let's go home."

The night air is agreeable as we ride back and I can't help but think about what she said. You see, Kaylee has never been too tired for any adventure, large or small. So what gives?

Then for some reason I start thinking that maybe it's the money. She's never before had any qualms about me spending money but this time it seems like she's, I don't know, worried about it for me. Now, when I go out on long rides, I always make sure I have more than enough coinage. But that doesn't mean I'm rich. I'm not. But I don't think she know that. Like I said, what gives?

We get back to her place and the lovemaking is immediate but, for whatever reason, slow and deep and deeply satisfying. While we're sitting on the couch – that's where we did the deed – I look around.

A thrift store coffee table. Old pictures of famous artwork covered with cracked glass in third-hand frames. A worn-out rug. A throwaway easy chair covered with a decades-old brown blanket. The couch is lumpy, the refrigerator's motor grinds, the kitchen and bathroom faucets leak, and the gas stove has to be lit with matches.

Other things, too. Other than three to-the-nines outfits that are starting to show wear, she doesn't have many clothes and most look like Salvation Army rejects. Her shoes are mostly old and worn and her jewelry is cheap. The blankets and sheets on her bed are hand-me-downs as are her bath towels. In fact, not only does she own only a little, just about everything she does own is flat out shabby or on its way there.

Further, she doesn't have many friends. Not because she's antisocial, she's not, but because she's always by herself painting. It's embarrassing that I'm noticing all this for the first time.

I remember some conversations we've had in the past about her everyday life and come to realize that the reason I spend so much money when I visit is because it's the only two or three days a year when she gets to get out and feel like she's an active part of society.

Again, I feel guilty. All this time I'd thought of her as nothing but a high-priced date, someone who insists on only the finest, and when I thought of the great sex, I always figured it was worth it.

But the reality is, the only things Kaylee really enjoys are painting, her paintings and a once-or-twice-a-year visit from a biker. I'd always thought of our relationship as her taking advantage of me, but now I'm thinking it's been the other way around.

With no preamble, I ask, "Kaylee, how far behind are you on your rent?"

She stiffens. "Six weeks."

"How much is it?"

"Six hundred."

"A month?"

She looks at her lap and nods.

"Any plans to get caught up?"

"This commission for four dog portraits from this old rich couple."

I think about that. She's a hell of an artist and describes her style as "Raphael with a dash of Renoir," but she's painting four dog portraits for rent money. It's not right. "How much?"

"Two hundred each."

"That still leaves you four hundred short. When will you get paid?"

"When they get back from Italy. Supposed to be in a month but last year they came home a week early, so I figured they'd come back two weeks early this time."

"That's only a hope, Kaylee. And even if they do come back in two weeks, you'll be three payments behind by then."

Her voice grows small. "I know."

I close my eyes and think about this stash of cash I always keep hidden in my bags. "Stay here." I come back then hand her two thousand dollars.

She doesn't reach for it and, honestly, looks forlorn. "What? You're paying me for sex now? I'm not a whore."

"No, you're not a whore." I wait. "I'm not paying you for anything. I'm giving it to you."

"I won't be able to pay you back."

"You don't have to pay me back. I'm giving it to you." I say something my dad told me a number of times. "Neither a borrower nor a lender be." I sigh. "It's one of my personal credos."

"Sounds like Benjamin Franklin."

"Hamlet, act one, scene three. Polonius is giving his son advice before he … never mind, doesn't matter. Just take it."

Her eyes are wet as she looks into mine. "Really?"

"Really. I want you to have it. We'll both feel better."

She takes the bills. I sit next to her then she folds into me crying.

———

The next day has a far different character from our usual. For one thing, Kaylee dresses casually (old, paint-covered sweat shirt and sweat pants) which is completely unfamiliar because during all the other times I've visited, she always dressed to impress. And she doesn't wear any makeup. (I never knew she had light freckles.) And she makes scrambled eggs, toast and coffee for breakfast. Never before have I seen her prepare any kind of meal.

After breakfast, I ask if she has any idea of what to do for the day. (Other than, you know, the sex thing.) She skews her bottom lip to the right, bites it and looks around. Finally she says, "Let's go for a ride. A long one." Well, that suits me just fine.

———

You know, there's something hidden-away and special about Kentucky's countryside. Sure, Louisville, Frankfort, and Lexington are big cities and everyone's heard about them. But it seems that in the countryside and especially the hills, those famous places are never considered, as if they don't exist or exist in another country. And a separate culture has been developing for hundreds of years, one of family, faith and fidelity.

Too, the trees and skies and waters reflect those virtues. I begin to consider that they're the genesis of them or, perhaps, they and those virtues began growing alongside one another some many years ago. However this part of the country came about, I don't know, but I do know it's a heart-filled place.

I decide we'll ride up to a place I've been wanting to visit for some time: Cave Run Lake. So we head east on side roads and highways and have coffee in Mt. Sterling. After we turn south on State Highway 801 is when we begin stopping often, the area being so laid-back and cozy.

It gets even more so when we head south on Pretty Ridge Road. Just after crossing North Fork Licking River – I love the names of these places! – we park in a turnout then walk down to a low rise that looks over a creek.

We sit next to each other, close, like two kernels on a cob, each of us in a contemplative mood. Quiet and peaceful. Every now and again, I throw my head back, half close my eyes, and catch a whiff of lilac.

I sometimes look at Kaylee's profile and wonder what her artist's eyes see, what they capture that I can't, and for the first time, I wonder what's in her heart.

Later, we turn onto Old Beaver Road heading into the sunset. Gentle and easy curves, trees like good neighbors, clouds like guardians of safety. Air that is new and full of gentle life.

———◦———

The last sliver of sun disappears as we roll into Frenchburg, so we get a room. Kaylee insists on a cheap one ("but clean!") so that's what I get. After unloading, I ask her what she wants for dinner. Again, she bites her lower lip. Other than this morning, I can't recall ever seeing her do that. Maybe it's a new quirk, maybe not, but it sure does sit at the top the cuteness scale.

"Taco Bell!"

I stare at her in disbelief. "Taco Bell? You want Taco Bell for dinner?"

"Yes! A burrito supreme and two soft tacos and a big root beer."

"Oh … kay. Wanna eat there or bring it back here?"

She thinks for a second. "There. You know, like we're on a date."

A date? At Taco Bell? With Kaylee? Well, she is who she is so she gets what she wants, right? "Well, okay. If you're as hungry as I am, we should get moving."

The funny thing is, when we get there it is like we're on a date. A first date. I'm nervous. So is she. We small-talk and laugh out loud at only moderately funny things. We sit up straight, napkins on the laps, say please and thank you, the works.

Kaylee is positively school-girl charming. Scrunches her nose at only a hint of something gross and becomes mock-shocked when I say something mildly risqué. I feel like I'm fifteen and it's the first time I've ever really talked with a girl.

When we get back to our room, it gets awkward. For me, anyway. We immediately plop on the bed then turn on the TV. (Huh?) We watch the Weather Channel, a little news, and two old episodes of Magnum, P.I. It's about midnight when we she heads off to the bathroom.

The thing is, I don't know what to do. Should I start with some foreplay? Treat her like a wench – she always loves it when I call her that – and have my way? Or kiss her on the cheek, say goodnight, then roll over and go to sleep? What?

My questions are answered when Kaylee steps out of the bathroom, fully naked. The one bedside lamp is but a warm glow, and coming through the partly open window is the scent of gardenias. She stands next to the bed in a bashful pose. Virginal. I reach up and bring her to me. We kiss and only kiss for the longest time. We fondle and it's electric. The love-making lasts an eternity.

The next six days are the likes of which I've never before experienced with any woman, especially Kaylee.

After we get back to her place, I immediately fall into my handyman persona. I fix both faucets, clean out the bottom of the refrigerator so we can barely hear it hum, and patch up the walls in the living room and paint them. Other stuff, too. And all the while we talk. Mostly about inconsequential stuff but occasionally about our deep-rooted beliefs.

I'm fixing the cord on one of her lamps when she asks, "What do you do for a living?"

"Electrician."

"Oh." She pauses as if she's somehow intruding." Where do you live?"

"Southern California."

She stares out the window. "Is it nice?"

"If you like too many people, outrageous taxes, and a cost of living that approaches the national debt."

166

She laughs. I stop working and look into the distance, a half-smile on my face. "Actually, it's jaw-dropping gorgeous when you get out of the cities. The ocean, the mountains. Weather's unbeatable. And so many world-class roads. Angeles Crest, Highway 33, Route 36, Rim of the World Highway, the Mighty 190. Man, it goes on and on.

"There's a stretch on the Pacific Coast Highway where, in early spring, you have a mountain on one side covered with wild flowers and a two hundred foot cliff on the other side that settles down to a dark-sand beach. Makes the ocean a color blue you've never seen before."

I look down and slowly shake my head. "Then there're the giant redwoods. There's a road in Northern California called the Avenue of the Giants that weaves right through thousands of them. It's like you're riding in front of gods.

"The other giant redwoods are in the Sierra Nevada in Central California and, I dunno, but they seem even bigger than their brothers up north. Did you know that a redwood's bark is fire resistant? Crazy to think about, but it's true."

I chuckle in disbelief. "One of them fell down years ago from a lightning strike and burned out from the inside and there's a photo of it from, I think, the '20s. That tree was so big that twenty-six horses are corralled inside the shell of it along with all the provisions for four dozen lumberjacks.

"But the biggest one is the General Sherman. It's five hundred years older than the bible and has enough wood to build forty homes."

Kaylee's mouth and eyes are wide with wonderment.

———∾———

For two and a half days, Kaylee insists on either going to Taco Bell for our meals or cooking them herself. That is, if you consider microwaving macaroni and cheese or seventy-nine cent pot pies as cooking, then yeah, she's cooking our meals.

But at dinnertime on the third night, I insist on going to a somewhat pricey Italian restaurant. Sure, she put up a bit of resistance but, all in all, it was an easy sell.

The restaurant's interior is an open-air type of setting. It's a welcoming atmosphere, the staff is Southern friendly, and we'd heard the food is excellent. There is, however, one unpleasant aspect.

The man is large in the waist, really large, sloppily dressed, in need of a shave, and sweat totally soaks the armpits of his old white shirt. Despite his sloppy appearance, he's evidently rich, something I gather

167

by the demeaning way he treats the staff and this pompous air he has about him. He sits cater-corner from us, alone. (Gee, I wonder why?)

Mr. Pompous' first insults were few and much like neanderthal grunts, but they soon become louder and more frequent and at least somewhat articulated.

When he "accidentally" pushes half his pasta salad on the floor and won't even move his feet when the busboy comes to clean it up, I put my full attention on him, basically staring and not reacting, though I admit he is getting under my skin.

The thing is, I admire food service workers. They're constantly on their feet, have to be friendly, and have to put up with guys like Mr. Pompous here. And I sincerely do not like those who treat them as underlings.

Anyway, Mr. Pompous notices me staring at him. "What're you looking at?"

I don't answer, don't even blink.

He scoffs then pushes more of his salad on the floor. "You like that?" He derisively laughs. Flicks more salad on the floor. More laughing. Still, I don't react. More salad. Keeps laughing and looks around to find others who share his twisted humor, but they all look away when he does.

He looks back at me with this evil dare-ya look and begins to throw bits of pasta toward Kaylee and me. He throws harder and harder and finally a pasta shell lands on Kaylee's shoulder. She has a hurt look that just about kills me.

Mr. Pompous is laughing loudly now and I can't recall ever seeing anything more ugly. I still don't react – outwardly, anyway – but I do owe it to Kaylee to put an end to this.

I grab a napkin then wipe the mess off her shoulder. I kiss her forehead then give her a wink. I turn and look at Mr. Pompous. He's still laughing, forcing it like a king's jester.

I walk straight over to him, no emotion showing, then deliver a downward haymaker to the left side of his face. The chair breaks, he's on the floor in a flash, unconscious, then the chair topples on top of him.

Damn, did that feel good!

The next day, it's time for me to head over to West Virginia to see my parents. It's mid-morning and I'm all packed and loaded up. We're standing on Kaylee's porch in a light embrace, lips within inches. It's difficult to not kiss her. But on the other hand, it's easy to just stand there and breathe in her sweetness.

I'm nervous, heart galloping like the winning horse on the last stretch of the Kentucky Derby. I clear my throat. "So, I was thinking that, I dunno, do you think that maybe, you know, it'd be okay with you if I, you know, stay in touch? You know, call you now and then?"

"Really?"

"Yeah! I mean if it's okay. Don't want to take you away from those puppy portraits."

She smiles. "How long will you be at your parent's."

"A week or so."

"Oh." She bites her lip again. "Your parents are good people?"

"The best."

"Mine died in a fire when I was twelve."

"Yeah, I know." I take a deep breath. "No brothers or sisters. Raised by your aunt and uncle. Lost your virginity on your sixteenth birthday. High school cheerleader. You hate scary movies, drunks and kale. Your top bowling score is 123. Your favorite book is Wuthering Heights.

"Decided not to go to college because 'teaching art is just a hustle.' Your style is 'Raphael with a dash of Renoir.' And your top bucket list item is to spend a week at the Musée d'Orsay in Paris."

She's shocked. "You remember all that?"

"All that and more, Kaylee." We fold into each other for a full minute, the hot air wrapping around us like a hooded parka. "So uh, would it be okay if I, you know, stay in touch?"

She jumps up and down. "Oh yes! Yes, yes, yes!"

"Well, okay then. That's what I'll do."

Two days later, I pull up in front of my parent's diner. It's an old wood-paneled building, freshly painted bright yellow, not large, with a ramp that leads up to the front door, on top of which is a hand-painted sign that reads, "The Rooster crows but the Hen delivers the goods."

A bell rings when I walk in. Dad's serving lunches and mom's in the kitchen. When they see me all three of our faces light up like the grand finale of Fourth of July fireworks.

I spend my days helping serve the diners when it's busy and doing a little carpentry work and electrical upgrades when it's not. And, of course, eating mom's amazing meals. Despite the work, I feel like I'm gaining three pounds a day.

Every evening after the diner is closed and cleaned up, the three of us go to their home, where we're greeted by their bloodhound puppy, Trigger, who eats everything. Couches, screwdrivers, rosemary bushes, doesn't matter.

We sit and talk about whatever. Mom keeps making sure I always ride safely, dad nods at her sage advice, and I tell them about all the places I've visited and the wild things that have happened.

One night the three of us play Scrabble. Mom wins. She always does. On another night, dad reads aloud the Edna St. Vincent Millay poem "Renascence," like he's done many times. And as it always happens, he can barely finish the last stanza because his eyes are filled with tears, satisfied tears. Mine and mom's, too.

> *The world stands out on either side*
> *No wider than the heart is wide;*
> *Above the world is stretched the sky, —*
> *No higher than the soul is high.*
> *The heart can push the sea and land*
> *Farther away on either hand;*
> *The soul can split the sky in two,*
> *And let the face of God shine through.*
> *But East and West will pinch the heart*
> *That can not keep them pushed apart;*
> *And he whose soul is flat — the sky*
> *Will cave in on him by and by.*

As I had said to Kaylee, my parents are the best.

Speaking of Kaylee, I don't ever mention her because, for some reason, I want her for only myself for as long as possible. I had decided to call her in the evenings, but though the time with my parents is as pleasant as pleasant can be, waiting for them to head off to bed at nine-thirty seems like it takes a year every day.

It's the fourth day of my visit and we've just sat down for our evening conversation. The sun has set and slivers of cool night air drift around us. Trigger licks my hand over and over and keeps trying to gnaw on my boots. Without preamble, mom asks, "What's her name?"

I freeze. Dad looks at me with eyes the same as mine. "Come on, son. Every night you're in your room talking and laughing on the phone for hours. We're not deaf, you know."

Mom raises her eyebrows. "Well?"

"Okay." I take a deep breath. "Her name's Kaylee. She lives in Lexington."

Mom asks, "Is she pretty?"

"Oh, yeah." I smile sheepishly. "Cute as a kitten in clover."

Dad, being my dad, asks, "How's the sex?"

Mom slaps the table. "The impertinence! Don't you dare ask our son a question like that!" She then gets a mischievous smile, raises one eyebrow, and looks at me out of the corners of her eyes. "So. Is she good in bed?"

Dad about falls out of his chair, laughing, my face is the color of a crimson rose, and mom is trying her hardest to not join in with dad's guffawing. Thankfully, the answer's obvious so I don't have to say a word.

That night, I relate the conversation to Kaylee. She laughs in her carefree way – I close my eyes and can actually see her bright eyes – then says, "God, I love your parents!"

Kaylee and I never have a conversation that lasts under two hours, a common subject being how, for six years, we had each misinterpreted who the other actually was.

Like I said, I'd always thought of her as nothing but a high-class chick who insisted on only the finest. She'd always thought of me as a sort of Mr. MoneyBags who also wanted only the finest and constantly downplayed his fortune.

The rest of the week passes by pretty much the same. Well, pretty much the same except for a longing to see Kaylee that grows and grows. Sometimes, I upbraid myself for never having actually realized Kaylee's true nature but mostly, I feel blessed. Blessed for having finally seen it.

Saying goodbye to my parents is bittersweet. I must have promised to visit them again at least a dozen times and hugged them each two dozen times. Wouldn't have it any other way.

The ride back to Lexington is bliss. The traffic is light, the warm air like a sweetheart's grasp, and the smells of lilacs and gardenias pull me forward, forward to that amazing and amazingly unique woman.

When I pull onto her driveway, she steps onto the porch and just stands there looking at me. Sweat pants and sweat shirt covered with splotches of paint, sleeves rolled up past her elbows. Hair in a ponytail. Sweet smile. Hands at her sides. Joyful. Eyes full of hope.

Kaylee.

END

LAST RIDE

My biggest regret, maybe the only one, is that I never got to really know them.

I was in the middle lane waiting at one of those big city red lights that last forever when they pulled up next to and behind me, side by side, in the right lane. The lead rider and I nodded to each other, then he leaned over and asked where I was headed.

I shrugged my shoulders because I didn't have a destination and hadn't thought about one. Just wanted to ride somewhere, get out of that traffic, which wasn't that bad, come to think of it, but still it was traffic, cars and a few trucks and, well, I wanted to get out of it and, after being in ya-gotta-wear-a-helmet California for six months, ride without a helmet. One of the wonderful things about Arizona.

He told me his name was Nelson and said they were going ride the 89 to Prescott then the 89A to Sedona. I smiled and pulled my head back a tad, as if to say, "Is that right?" Then he said I was welcome to join them if I wanted. I nodded and smiled again. "Sounds good. Think I will."

He then gave me that guy nod, the one where the chin goes down once, eyes half closed, lips pressed together, as if to say, "Alright, we got a deal." From just that short exchange, I felt we had gotten to know each other, two men part of the same brotherhood.

Next to Nelson was a tall blond woman, who I took to be his lady. About my age, nice smile. Attractive. Seemed comfortable on her bike but not quite old school comfortable. She and Nelson never looked at each other but, somehow, there was an understanding, a connection between them, palpable almost.

I looked at her again and she reminded me of my sixth grade school teacher, Mrs. Phillips. It occurred to me, right then, that I was the same age as Mrs. Phillips was when I was her student. Interesting, because I never thought I'd be the same age as she was back then. She'd always be the same age, I'd always be younger and look up to her. Take everything she said as a fact.

Sixth grade was my worst year socially but my best year for realizing who I wanted to be. Mrs. Phillips gave up her own lunchtime in the teacher's lounge just so four of us oddball characters could congregate in her classroom. There was Alison, Allie, Reese and me.

We'd talk about whatever came up as long as it didn't have anything to do with the goings-on at school. Except for Reese. He'd just sit at his desk all the time not saying a word.

This had been the routine for a month or so when, out of the blue, Reese came up to me and said, "Got two acres behind the house, all dirt. My dad lets me ride dirt bikes. Wanna come over?" I said I did and that Saturday was the first time I rode a motorcycle.

Reese was useless when it came to teaching me how to ride, so every ten or so yards I'd spin out or the tires would slip or the front wheel would go hard right or left and I'd go down. Finally, his dad came out and taught me the nuts and bolts of it all. Did pretty good after that. Had fun. So much fun that I went over to Reese's three or four times a week.

The thing was, I never got the feeling that Reese, or his dad for that matter, liked me much. It was like all of it, the riding and the cleaning off of mud and putting the gear and bikes away, was nothing but a series of mundane tasks. Like brushing your teeth or cleaning out your toe jam.

But thinking about it now, I believe that, in their own way, they were friendly, that they were just loners and not skilled in the arts of social graces.

After that school year ended, Reese and I fell out for some reason. No fight or arguments or anything. I just stopped going over there and he stopped expecting me to.

A few weeks later, I fell in with some bike jocks. Older kids who looked at dirt riding as a competition and a reason to boast. During that summer vacation, their dads would drive us out to the countryside three or four or five times a week and we'd pretend like we were Supercross champions.

Their self-praising bravado stuff quickly got old but it didn't matter because I was hooked and would do anything to get on two wheels. For some reason, maybe the difference in ages, I always figured they weren't real friends but in actual fact, they were. I mean, I knew their girlfriends and their sisters and brothers and their parents. Their dogs, too. Even had dinner at their homes a few times.

Hitting the dirt three to five days a week was bliss. But, as with all things in life, it came to an end when school started up. For a week or so I felt like I was alone in the world. And that's when my dad came to the rescue.

He'd been a Harley rider when he met my mom. They rode a lot for a year or so but when she got pregnant with me, they settled down, got regular jobs and ended up selling the bike. But with them, like most everyone else, they never lost the longing for the rumble of an engine, and when it became clear I was committed to it, too, they bought me a used Honda 350 and my dad got an old Harley Ironhead.

The bikes didn't look like much but it didn't matter. Riding with my dad was the first time I felt the brotherhood that's common to bikers. I was too young to go to a tavern with him but he'd let me have a sip or two of beer at the end of a ride. I never got a buzz but it did make me feel a little grown up. Loved him for that. Loved him for a lot of other things, too.

There's not one curve on this road. Not even a slight one. Don't come across that too often. And it's stretching out forever. The weird thing is that, despite the straight-as-a-ruler aspect, it feels good to ride it. Like I could go on forever, too.

Behind Nelson and his lady were two riders who were obviously another tight couple. Obvious because they, too, had an almost palpable connection. I instantly liked them, partly because the woman looked a little like my mom. Pretty, a little over five feet tall, long and wavy black hair, kind face.

Riding with my mom and dad – she always rode on the back – was a completely different experience from riding with just my dad. Mom was the always-prepared one and would always pack water, juice, jerky, and trail mix. And at the end of the day, my dad wouldn't even think of giving me a sip of beer.

It was fine, though, because we both knew mom had the higher moral standards and we loved her for it. Like my dad often said, "She keeps me in line and I'm a better man for it." It's interesting, the different ways you learn about life.

I finally got my driver's license when I was sixteen and got the motorcycle part of it as soon as I could. It was a proud day for me when it came in the mail because, right there, it said M1.

For high school graduation, we sold our bikes. My parents and I split the cost of a used Harley 883 and my dad bought a used Electra Glide. And that's when we began riding with other families.

It was never a formal gathering; those who could make it would, and those who couldn't, wouldn't. Sometimes we'd end up at a location that actually had a name and was built for resting. Other times, we'd just sit in the dirt at a turnout. Didn't matter, really.

The best ride we ever did lasted three days and two nights. There were four couples and five of us kids. We took off in the morning, rode Interstate 5 over the Grapevine and into California's Central Valley and spent the night at Lake Isabella. The next day, we went north on Mountain Highway, then took the M-50 and the M-90 to the Mighty 190.

Now, was that something! The spanking fresh air, the mountains and cliffs, and the tree-lined surroundings wouldn't quit. Neither would the curves. One after another, as if the engineers who designed it had never heard of a straight line.

There was that one blind curve just after Johnsondale where every one of us barely missed a branch that covered the right two-thirds of the road. I came close to smashing into the rider in front of me and later, when I mentioned it to my dad, he said, "That's why you don't follow too close on the curves." Lesson learned.

To be honest, though, I got tired of curve after curve pretty quickly. Got to the point where all I wanted was a mile stretch where I could crank the throttle, maybe get into third gear for once. From the conversations when we pulled over to take photos and stretch the legs, it seemed to be a common sentiment between us kids.

I learned another lesson at the end of that day. We were all sitting in this huge jacuzzi at a motel in Porterville and the parents were talking about how great a curvy canyon is, that that's where you can tell a real rider from an amateur. The five of us kids kept looking at each other, getting a little more self-conscious as the conversation wore on.

After that, I started looking for curves and found some great ones to practice on. Little Tujunga, Decker, Red Box, and on and on. Dad showed me the ins and outs of it all – God, I loved that guy! – and together we took an advanced motorcycle course. Afterward, I bought a used R-6 and took it out to the California Motorcycle School. Those instructors were amazing. Learned a lot there, too.

The other sport bike riders were helpful and encouraging, and I made good friends. But the thing is, it's a different type of camaraderie than the big bike riders have, and the fellowship among cruisers and baggers suited me better.

Man, this nighttime desert air is the best. And there's no traffic at all. Road's in great shape, too. It keeps going straight as a pushrod, but for the first time in I-don't-know-how-many years, the lack of curves isn't bothering me at all. Can't tell how far away those hills are, but I think I'll keep going till I get to the other side of them where that glow of lights is. Most likely a small, quiet town. A good place to settle down for the night.

I turned around again and looked at the third and fourth couples. They were riding two-up and each couple was like one. A blend of comfort and trust and love and history together. They all smiled and the women waved. Made me feel like I'd known them for years and I immediately wished I had a lady sitting on the back.

I've had a number of girlfriends over the years. A few weren't into riding, most were, but I never found that special one. The one who knows you inside-out and your every move so well that it's like having an extra set of hands on the handlebars.

I looked in my rearview mirror again. The way one of the gals was dressed, black boots, tight jeans, and a revealing top, reminded me of a girlfriend I had in the last semester of my senior year in high school.

Man, was Rachel sweet! She absolutely loved riding on the back, something her mother disapproved of but was nice enough to not forbid. Her parents were white-collar rich and though my family was

177

blue-collar, they were civil to me. Nevertheless, I could always tell they wanted "someone better" for their daughter.

They insisted Rachel go to an ivy league college back east after high school. For us, the thought of being apart was as sad as sad could be. When it was time for her to head out, we broke up in a bittersweet way. No hard feelings at all, just tears and well-wishes.

After Rachel got settled in college, she started riding with one of those guys who likes doing wheelies on the freeway at a hundred and ten. One evening, they hit a side rail of the Pennsylvania Turnpike. The guy came away with nothing but some cuts and bruises, but Rachel was in the hospital for two weeks in a coma.

I went to visit her. The night before she died, she woke up, looked at me and smiled, tears in her eyes. "I knew you'd come. I love you. You're the best." I'll never forget her. Funny that I'd never thought of it before now but, looking back, I believe that I did have "That One" in Rachel.

The scariest thing was the sound. The metallic screech. The coupling breaking, the cab on its side, the axles stretched to the breaking point. It all seemed to take forever, every millisecond a lifetime. And there was nowhere to go, nothing to do but watch and wait for the inevitable.

Behind those two couples were three solo riders. The first was a gal with a long ponytail riding what looked like an old Heritage, the other two were guys on Dynas, but I couldn't make out the models. Even with my sunglasses on, they all could tell when I looked at them in my mirrors and would nod in that biker way that Nelson had: half-smile, chin down once.

The last one, a roly-poly guy in all black, looked a little like my best buddy from my first two high school years. Billy was an army brat originally from Georgia and didn't look like much of an athlete but, damn, could he play basketball. Whipped my butt a bunch and I was one of the best. He joined the junior varsity team but the coach never really gave him a chance – "He doesn't look like a basketball player" – so Billy quit after his first season.

Even though he was too young to get a driver's license, Billy rode to school every day on a ratty, 125cc Kawasaki Eliminator with no license plates. To me, he was the coolest. I can't begin to count the number of times we went hunting with bows and arrows, or walked a couple of miles to a creek and fished.

Of all the friends I've had over the years, and I've had a lot, I have to say Billy was maybe the most fun to be around. Always a smile and never an antagonistic attitude. Well, except when he'd beat the snot out of one or two other students who deserved it.

That cement truck must have been going over sixty when the driver hit the brakes too hard and it started to skid, turned to its left then fell onto its right side, coming straight at us. A total of three seconds at the most. After that? Don't really remember much. The heat, a few screams, darkness, then silence.

There are advantages to riding alone. You can speed up or slow down at your whim, pull over wherever, cover a lot of miles or only a few, and whenever you want you can take a long rest or no rest at all. It's a good way, maybe the best way, to find out whom you've made yourself out to be.

But then, there are advantages to riding with a group, too. The camaraderie is the most obvious. The sharing of water, trail mix, and jerky. A good meal, a fine brew, and a game of pool at the end of a day. The practical jokes, the ribbing, the laughter.   The hugs and pats on the back. Probably the most valuable advantage being the ever-growing trust and faith you have with others.

It was that trust and faith that I was looking forward to the most when I agreed to ride with Nelson and the rest of them. I'd been a loner for those six months in California so I figured it was time to get some of that back into my life. I wasn't worried about any unhappy consequences because, in my experience, the overwhelming majority of bikers are good folks.

Now that I think about it, though, trust and faith in others have been a constant part of my life, even in California. And I just now realized that it all starts with trust and faith in yourself, something I learned from my dad and mom. And from Rachel, too. And from all the guys and gals I've ridden with.

What is it with this road? It's like joy is part of the asphalt. I guess that's why the no-curves-ness of it isn't bothering me. And this weather is paradise. That soft glow on the other side of those mountains has to be from a quiet and peaceful place. Whatever it's called, I think maybe I'll stay there for a while.

The mountains seem a bit closer and the lights in my rearview mirrors have all but disappeared so I guess this road will end sometime. I mean, everything ends sometime, right? Even friendships and people. Like how I ended up not hanging out with Reese any more, or with any of those dirt bike and sport bike friends I'd made. Or like that summer when Billy moved away. Or like when I was a kid and thought my mom and dad were ageless, would be around forever. Rachel, too.

Yeah, I'm thinking that that quiet and peaceful place on the other side of those mountains is exactly what I've been looking for. The perfect place to end my ride.

END

TWO ACTORS, A BUILDING, AND A RIOT

I'd always wanted to write. Worked on it now and again throughout my life but didn't really start in earnest until somewhere around 1996-97. My first short stories were, well, like most anyone's first short stories, meaning they fell into the nice-try-keep-working-at-it category.

This one, "Two Actors, a Building, and a Riot," was the first one I felt was worthy of publication. I started it in, I think, 1998-99 and finished it in 2002, though, as is my wont, kept polishing it up now and again over the next many years.

It's not a biker story. Nor is it fiction. Rather it's about something that actually happened in New York City back in 1849. If you're not aware of it, your jaw will drop.

THE PLAYERS

WILLIAM CHARLES MACREADY (1793-1873) was an English actor whose favorite role (or should I spell that favourite?) was Macbeth. He studied law at Rugby and intended a profession as a barrister, but just before taking the bar exam, encountered financial difficulties and instead pursued a career as an actor and theater owner, just like his father.

He actually disliked the profession but, being a determined sort with visions of greatness, decided upon a mission to raise the social status of the actor and elevate theater art in general.

Essentially, Macready accomplished his goals and, in fact, was the first actor ever to be knighted. He was also one of the first to demand full rehearsals with the goal in mind of having the entire production flow as a seamless whole.

Prior to this, actors would learn their lines on their own, never rehearse together, and when on stage would declaim to the audience rather than interact with each other. Macready's methods led to the creation of the stage manager, which later led to the creation of the director. (I'll let all you actors decide if this was a good thing or not.)

To the displeasure of many of his fellow actors, Macready was a taskmaster and perfectionist. He would endlessly drill all nuances of a performance, all the way down to the proper bend of finger. His own acting style was cerebral and intense, and he was considered to be the second greatest actor of his era; Edmund Kean, by most contemporary accounts, being the greatest.

EDWIN FORREST (1806-1872) was a self-taught American actor. Everything about him and his life was the opposite of Macready's – for one thing, he was quite handsome – except for the fact that he worked on his craft every bit as diligently, though in very different ways. Through a strict regimen of diet and exercise, he built for himself an imposing physique. In fact, he is credited with starting the tradition of ruggedly built, handsome and heroic leading men, and he almost never played a villain.

Perhaps the biggest difference between the two men was that Forrest's acting style was physical rather than cerebral and many, one of whom was Walt Whitman, criticized his ranting and stormily declaiming ways. Drama critic William Winter of the New York Tribune once described him as "a vast animal, bewildered by a grain of genius." (Ah critic! To what extremes thou wilt go to harvest a grain of wit!)

Forrest was fiercely patriotic and always eager to tell everyone (loudly, of course) about the superiority of the American Way: humble beginnings, hard work, unbridled success. Further, he abhorred all aristocratic manner, especially British. His fans, and there were legions of them, were primarily working class folk and he was their champion

ASTOR PLACE OPERA HOUSE opened for business in 1847 with the idea that its graceful design and luxurious appointments would provide a suitable venue for the finest art. It sat, splendidly, on the corner of Broadway and the Bowery in New York City. At the time, Broadway was lined with the large homes of the wealthy while the Bowery was, well, the Bowery: boarding houses, saloons and brothels.

The crème de la crème policies of Astor Place – for one thing, part of the dress code was white kid gloves and white silk tie – irked some of the egalitarian-minded denizens of the Bowery. Nevertheless, the dress code was often ignored and many of them attended events at Astor Place sitting next to their wealthy neighbors. For the first year and a half of its operation, Astor Place Opera House enjoyed a peaceful and healthy business.

ACT I

In 1836, at the age of thirty, Forrest traveled to England to study with Edmund Kean. (Remember, Kean was the only actor most everyone thought greater than Macready.) Later that year, he made his first appearance in a leading role as Othello in New York City and was an immediate success.

His success continued unabated for eight more years. Then in 1845, he returned to England, this time heralded as The Great American Shakespearean Actor. Well, it didn't go well. Simply put, he got bad reviews. A lot of them.

Now, for some reason, and no one knows how or why, he got it into his head that Macready was behind all the bad press. Not one to back down, he traveled to Edinburgh to attend a Macready performance of Hamlet during which he actually hissed the actor. (You can only imagine how loudly.)

This outraged the British Press, and Macready as well, I suppose. When interviewed, Forrest defended his questionable behavior saying that it was the audience's right and, more so, their duty to give an actor "on-the-spot critiques." The British Press and public were not convinced and any hopes he had of success in England vanished forever.

Forrest came home carrying a grudge as big as his biceps, and when his fans heard of his reception in England, his celebrity status became married to that of martyr. As you can imagine, this significantly helped his career.

Now he could do no wrong, could make no misstep, could not rant too loudly nor flex too boldly. (Except for some of the critics, of course.)

Every performance he gave was to overflowing, adoring crowds and he began to make the unheard of sum of two thousand dollars a week. (Remember, this was in the 1830s and 1840s.) Forrest was King and he ruled America.

If only the story ended here.

ACT II

Macready had always wanted to live in the United States after his retirement so in 1848, he launched his third and final tour of the states – the first two were in 1826 and 1843 – with an eye to finding a suitable place to do so. When he arrived, the press gave him a cold reception and there were rumors of retaliation from Forrest supporters, who had long since become convinced that Macready was behind the bad reviews Forrest had gotten in England.

One of Macready's first appearances was at Astor Place in the fall of 1848. Despite the dire predictions, however, everything went smoothly, the press warmed up to him, and everyone was happy and looked forward to his tour across the United States. Except Forrest. He was still nursing that grudge and those biceps, and he decided on a course of revenge.

What he did was this. Whenever Macready performed, Forrest would stage his own production of the same play in the same city on the same night. Further, he personally undertook the publicity campaign of publicly announcing these opposing performances along with writing inflammatory, anti-Macready letters to the local newspapers. (You must admit, he had a big set of – how shall I put this delicately? – gonads.)

Immediately, Forrest fans started the habit of attending Macready's productions (maybe they couldn't find a seat at the Forrest productions?) with the hope that their loud and coarse "on-the-spot critiques" would make things uncomfortable for him, which they most likely did.

As the double tour crossed the United States, this habit quickly became a tradition and Macready could never enjoy a peaceful night of Shakespeare. Nevertheless, he remained undaunted and aloof from it all.

He had always felt Americans to be "rather boorish" anyway – I can just hear him say that: heavy, drawn-out British accent with nose in air – and I guess this behavior helped to prove him right, at least in his mind. Besides, he was getting better reviews than Forrest.

ACT III

In the spring of 1849, both Macready and Forrest arrived back in New York City. On May 7th, Macready appeared for a second run at Astor Place in the role of Macbeth while Forrest's production took place at the Broadway Theatre just a few blocks away.

There was even a third production of Macbeth that night: Thomas Hamblin decided to get into the act (sorry, overused pun) and staged his own production at the Bowery Theatre, also only a few blocks away. These were the three leading theaters in New York City but on that night, Astor Place was the center of attention.

Inside, the Forrest rabble-rousers were in fine form. In his diary, Macready wrote

> Copper cents were thrown, some struck me, four or five eggs, a great many apples, nearly – if not quite – a peck of potatoes, lemons, pieces of wood, a bottle of asafoetida [a gem resin] which splashed my own dress, smelling, of course, most horribly.

During the third act, four wooden chairs were thrown from the corner of the balcony, one of them shattering at Macready's feet. Wisely, he stopped his performance, pointed to the splinters around him, bowed, and left the stage.

This was big news. Really big news. As you would expect, the Astor Place managers, William Niblo and James H. Hackett, wanted to capitalize on all the free publicity and get Macready to do another performance.

Understandably, he wasn't keen on the idea, so Niblo and Hackett wrote and circulated a petition urging all connoisseurs of fine art to not back down from those "Forrest Ruffians." Many leading citizens signed it including Washington Irving, Herman Melville and Mayor Caleb S. Woodhull, who had been in office for only a week, poor soul.

Niblo and Hackett then covered all the windows with one and a half inch wooden planks and demanded protection from Mayor Woodhull, who promised the presence of about 250 policemen.

They then sold and gave away many more tickets than they had seats to fill in the hopes of having a 100% Macready crowd. As a counter move, the politician Captain Isaiah Rynder, later of Tammany Hall infamy, bought a number of tickets and gave them to Forrest supporters.

In the 1840s, the police were unarmed so Mayor Woodhull, wanting to cover his derrière, put the armed National Guard on alert. (Is this

185

incredible or what!) With all this in place, Macready was convinced he would be safe and agreed to another performance.

ACT IV

On 10 May 1849 at 8:00pm, the curtains raised on Macready's Macbeth with the Forrest minority booing loudly, the Macready majority applauding resoundingly.

However, the real drama was unfolding outside. Astor Place had become surrounded by 10-15,000 (yes, ten to fifteen thousand!) over-zealous Forrest supporters. They began by throwing stones at the doors and windows of Astor Place and, incredibly, the 250 policemen.

The police issued a warning for them to stop, the Forest ruffians ignored it and, instead, went to a nearby construction site, armed themselves with pieces of brick and pavement, and continued their assault. After the Forrest supporters ignored another warning, the police called in two divisions of the National Guard's 7th Regiment.

Soon, the Forrest rioters had shattered the wooden planks over Astor Place's windows and were pelting the audience inside along with the policemen and, believe it or not, the 7th Regiment, who were armed with guns, mind you.

The 7th Regiment fired a warning volley over the crowd but this made them think they were firing blanks, so they continued their brickbat barrage. The soldiers fired a second volley at ground level, but the onslaught continued unabated. They then fired a third, and final, volley directly into the crowd.

When it was all over, there were twenty-three people dead and over one hundred wounded. Predating the Civil War by twelve years, this was the first time in US history that American troops had fired upon and killed fellow Americans.

EPILOGUE

The crooked fingers of blame pointed everywhere: at Macready for starting the whole thing in England; at Forrest for fomenting hatred of Macready; at the newspapers for festering a petty feud between two actors; at Niblo, Hackett and the petitioners for hankering for another performance; at Mayor Woodhull for calling in armed troops; and on and on and on.

The blame finding, as you may expect, accomplished nothing beneficial and did nothing to assuage a city and country in shock and grief over more deaths than the Battle of New Orleans and the Boston Massacre combined.

Macready managed to slip out of Astor Place in disguise. He stayed at a friend's house that night and the next morning, in a closed carriage, traveled to New Rochelle where he boarded a train for Boston.

A few days later, he began his voyage back to England fearful that he would never be fully accepted by the British aristocracy – he never was – and could never fulfill his dream of retiring in the United States. His last performance was not quite two years later in the role of Macbeth.

Forrest's career slid precipitously after the Astor Place Riot, though he still had fans in the Bowery and a few other spots in the US. In 1851, he sued his wife, actress Catherine Sinclair, for divorce on the grounds of adultery. He lost the case as there was really no evidence – reminiscent of Othello, perhaps? – but continued appealing the decision for the next eighteen years.

The lawsuit ruined what little remained of his reputation and in 1872, he died, alone, in his huge Philadelphia mansion. He bequeathed most of his fortune to build a retirement home for actors.

Astor Place also suffered substantially from the riot. Niblo and Hackett, and the managers who succeeded them, tried everything from minstrel and magic shows to opera but could never make ends meet.

In 1854 it was turned into a lecture hall and in 1855 the name was changed to Clinton Hall and it became the home to the Mercantile Library of New York. In 1890, the original building was torn down and the new eleven-story Clinton Hall was built in its place.

After the Mercantile Library moved in 1932, Clinton Hall became the home to various businesses and sundry activities until 1995 when it was converted to condominiums.

Back in the early 1900s, Clinton Hall had been considered prestigious enough to have its own subway entrance so in 1904, Astor Place Station was built next to and under it.

Today, the only physical reminder of the Astor Place Riot is that very Astor Place Station situated in the triangle created by East 8th Street, Lafayette Street, and 4th Avenue.

END

ACKNOWLEDGEMENTS

Writing is an alone-activity, sure, but that doesn't mean that when the time for actually creating a book arrives, others don't get involved. They do. And it's a good thing they do.

I can write the book, yes, but all the other bric-a-brac? The things that must be done to create an actual book? To make it available to the public? If it were up to me alone, left to only my own wiles, I'd be in the proverbial "uhhh..." forever.

I consider the following trusted folks my friends, my exceptionally good friends, who never fail to keep me grounded and somewhat sane. Geniuses all.

WT Smith is a kindred spirit, a damn good man, and a helluva biker. He's read everything I've published and, I believe, even some pieces I haven't. His advices have never pointed me in a wrong direction and I'm smart enough to always take them sincerely.

Jody Ammerman is a valued genius. I almost always take to heart her suggestions on my scribblings. Like everyone else on this page, she makes my writing better and I truly thank her for it.

Ron Kule, Nick Howarth, Bryan Hall, JoJo Zawawi, and Carol Worthey are fellow authors. Exquisite wordsmiths all.

George Gluchowski, my publisher, is the amalgam of an ancient wise man and a benevolent godfather. Christa Echo Mella is the supreme designer of this book. (Without her, it would look like a discarded newspaper sitting at the bottom of a twenty-year-old dumpster.) Don Giannatti, a world class photographer (a helluva writer, too!), authored the photos that flawlessly grace the front and back covers. Am I lucky or what?!

Amber Gosling, Linda Ferguson, and Glenis Batley are as aesthetically trustworthy as anyone could be. All three are exemplary.

My three kids, Khalin, Lacee, and Jasmine, along with my four grandkids, Travis, Diego, Ana, and Vienna, are so, so interwoven into my life. I am blessed.

Last, but certainly not least, is Rose, the finest of ladies.

WHO IS FOSTER KINN?

Foster Kinn is a pseudonym for Dwight Bernard Mikkelsen. He was born and bred in Visalia, California, which is smack dab in the middle of the state's San Joaquin Valley. He is the son and brother of Danish immigrants, the father of three, and the grandfather of four. He describes himself as "fundamentally a freedom guy, a Classical music composer, and a not-too-bad raconteur who never has enough time to ride my motorcycle."

Speaking of motorcycles, Foster averages 15-20,000 riding miles a year and has ridden in all 50 states of the United States, 7 Canadian provinces and one Canadian territory. And he did all those miles with the same motorcycle, the same helmet, and the same pair of boots. (He often jokes, "And with the way I smell sometimes, you'd think I did it all with the same pair of socks!")

These travels are recounted in his first two books, *Freedom's Rush* and *Freedom's Rush II*, which are Amazon Bestsellers.

His third book is the highly acclaimed novel, *The Poet, the Professor, and the Redneck*, which was released in the summer of 2020.

He has been a professional musician and composer his entire adult life and has arranged or orchestrated for many artists including Quincy Jones, Barbra Streisand, Chicago and Whitney Houston. He has also worked on hundreds of films and TV shows.

His primary musical love, however, is Classical with a particular interest in ballet. His two full length, orchestral ballets, *Thumbelina* and *The Legend of Jack Frost* have never failed to delight all ages.

Visit Foster's website! www.FosterKinn. com.